THI

TRANSLATED BY NATALIA HERO

A NOVEL

Thirty
Copyright © Marie Darsigny, 2018
Translation Copyright © Natalia Hero, 2023

ISBN 978-1-988355-28-3
All rights reserved

Published by Metatron Press
Montreal, Quebec
www.metatron.press

Printed in Canada
First printing

Cover art © Studio Gabarit
Collages © Marie Darsigny, 2018

Originally published in French by © Les Éditions du remue-ménage

Library and Archives Canada Cataloguing in Publication

Title: Thirty / Marie Darsigny.
Other titles: Trente. English
Names: Darsigny, Marie, 1986- author.
Description: Translation of: Trente.
Identifiers: Canadiana 20230150691 | ISBN 9781988355283 (softcover)
Classification: LCC PS8607.A7525 T20813 2023 | DDC C843/.6—dc23
Classification: LCC PS3611.E3757 C56 2023 | DDC 811/.6—dc23

THIRTY

MARIE DARSIGNY

Translated from French by

NATALIA HERO

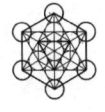

Metatron Press

THIRTY

JULY 7
AUGUST 23
SEPTEMBER 33
OCTOBER 43
NOVEMBER 57
DECEMBER 69
JANUARY 79
FEBRUARY 87
MARCH 105
APRIL 117
MAY 127
JUNE 143

JULY

I HAVEN'T WRITTEN ANYTHING in a week, I haven't written anything since I turned twenty-nine. I'm in a literary desert, a complete drought, I should also mention that I've stopped drinking, but that's another story. At times during this empty week I may have thought of words, beginnings of sentences even formed inside my head, I felt a spark of inspiration, but then, when I finally managed to formulate them, I realized it was something Elizabeth Wurtzel had already written. If it wasn't Elizabeth, it was Nelly, or Marie-Sissi, I don't know anymore, my muses are many, but often interchangeable, I call them by their first names and I end up forgetting who said what after repeating their words like litanies. The sad truth is that my favourite muses are depressed, it's true in English with Angelina Jolie and Elizabeth Wurtzel, but it's true in

French too with Nelly Arcan and Marie-Sissi Labrèche: dead or depressed. I've been twenty-nine for a week and I've been told, "it'll pass, you'll see," but I wonder what will pass exactly, everything passes, but nothing goes right for me because all I do is hit a wall. Nelly said it best: "Very early on I understood that in life, one must be happy; ever since, I've lived under pressure."[1] The pressure paralyzes me, makes me limp, a worm, by the way on the day of my twenty-ninth birthday I lay starfished on my bed, twenty-nine years of staring at the ceiling, I waited before making a decision. It's always complicated with me and decisions, whether it's choosing an ice cream flavour (Dairy Queen employees hate me) or whether to live or die (the people who love me will end up hating me from worrying so much). So I made the non-decision to go be a starfish elsewhere, at my mom's, twenty-nine-year-old little girl still sandwiched between her two parents. As I lay like a starfish I fell asleep and I wanted to sleep for eternity, but I was uncomfortable: my comforter made my thighs itch, or maybe it was mosquitoes. I quoted Fiona

---

1. Nelly Arcan, *Folle*, Paris, Seuil, 2004, p. 48.

Apple in my head: **I'M GOOD AT BEING UN-COMFORTABLE SO I CAN'T STOP CHANGING ALL THE TIME**, years spent searching for ways to get better, then I quoted Elizabeth Wurtzel out loud: **I AM ALWAYS TRYING TO GO TO THAT IMAGINARY SOMEWHERE OR TO GET TO THAT IMAGINARY SOMETHING, MY LIFE HAS BEEN ONE LONG LONGING**, an entire life spent waiting for something to happen, but what exactly. All throughout that first day of July when I turned 29, people wished me happy birthday several times, but as of tomorrow and for the next three hundred and sixty four days everyone will move on while my mind will endlessly remind me that time is passing. My mind doesn't wish me happy birthday, it tells me things like: "You're ugly and plain and old and stupid and you haven't accomplished anything, Elizabeth Wurtzel already had a best-seller under her belt at your age." My brain keeps a constant countdown, a timer before the sauce boils, before it splatters across the walls. After lying like a starfish long enough, I went back home, thanks mom the grass was soft, thanks mom my glass of water was cold, thanks mom your words were nice and finally thanks mom for bringing me into the world, it isn't your fault that you have a crab-daughter, a seaside Cancer. I went back home in my 1998 Saturn that's still running, ten years driving a car that sometimes acts as a refuge for crying on the road where no one can see me, it's more private than in the metro, although I'm also an expert at crying in the metro, I'm an expert at crying in public in general, expert at crying for an audience like Angelina Jolie in *Gia*, like any pretty girl in film that lets her tears fall without wincing or sniffling. So, I drove: Madonna tape, McDonald's, Esso, Fiona Apple tape, then I was home again. I told myself, "I'm twenty-nine years old," and I cried over my fate, my karma, my destiny that I don't understand, I cried over my life of twenty-nine years of birthdays, which were perfect up until now. "The fireworks are for you Marie," that's what they would say to me every 1st of July, I got fireworks, I got homemade cake, I got what every middle class child could ever want. At eighteen, I had a surprise party in my parents' backyard with alcohol they bought for me even though I was now old enough to buy it myself. At nineteen,

I got arrested, and I cried until my eyes were as red as the Canadian flag. On my twentieth, I had matchstick arms and they wanted to feed me with a cake that had my name on it. To celebrate my friends' effort I ate, even though I hadn't been. For my twenty-first, I discovered mojitos and I wanted to go to Chez Parée but no one wanted to come with me, so I kissed my best friend and went to bed. At twenty-two, I decided that I was old enough to party in the U.S. I saw fireworks there too, but not exactly on my birthday, three days later, for their birthday, then in New York with Marina Abramovic I cried, I told you: I cry all the time. For my twenty-third birthday I threw a sweet sixteen because everyone loves youth and party hats, everyone loves taking too many drugs and drinking too much alcohol only to end up crying at seven in the morning about how our calves are too small, that it's an aberration and no one will ever love us. For my twenty-fourth I covered my walls in silver wrapping paper, like in Warhol's Factory, that man-child that I hate, #TeamSolanas although that might be going a little too far, I like to repeat that "Life in this society being, at best, an utter bore and no aspect of society being at all relevant to women, there remains to civic-minded, responsible, thrill-seeking females only to overthrow the government, eliminate the money system, institute complete automation and destroy the male sex,"[2] and at my festive party à la Warhol I invited my girl friends over to watch me drink champagne, hiccupping out of fear of soon reaching a quarter century. My twenty-fifth was by far the most memorable, a party still unmatched, because there was magic, Sharpies, and a bar that has since closed: I'm keeping it a secret. My twenty-sixth birthday, on the other hand, was kind of boring, all I wanted was a poutine so I went to Rapido, which has also since closed. At Rapido I discovered that poutine could be disappointing, because everything is disappointing when you have a negative outlook. For my twenty-seventh I demanded that everyone dress in head-to-toe denim, Canadian tuxedo, we cooked things on the barbecue even though I don't like meat, I made an exception and washed it down with Miller Lime, a torrent of beer for the

---

2. Valerie Solanas, *SCUM Manifesto*, New York, Olympia Press, 1968, p. 2.

fallen vegetarian. For my twenty-eighth I locked myself in the bathroom where I had hidden a book beforehand underneath the sink, a special book, a worn out novel with traces of white powder on it. I'm far from a role model, hide your kids, it's not going to get any better with age. And there you have it, finally I get to twenty-nine, my twenty-ninth birthday was a week ago and I haven't written anything since, or maybe just this little piece, to say that I'm now getting dangerously close to my thirtieth birthday. If I could go back in time I'd smile at my mom, I'd smile at my dad, I'd smile at my friends who came over to my place on the day of my twenty-ninth birthday to watch me act stupid, if I could go back, I would just try to be a good girl, the kind of **GOOD GIRL** that Drake sings about, but we all know that **GOOD GIRL** doesn't exist, it's a lie, a myth, a mirage in the desert of femininity. "The good girl is, essentially, a trope that's used in an attempt to reign in a disruptive woman, or one that's threatening to the patriarchal version of what is and is not acceptable lady behavior. It's mansplaining feminine social etiquette. And it's infantilizing in its insistence in referring to grown ass women as 'girls.'"[3] I have nothing against the use of the word *girl* instead of *woman*, it suits me just fine to possess eternal youth, I want to get MISS tattooed on my forehead and GOOD GIRL on my chest, I want to be a good girl who will go on to become a good mother or a good wife. I JUST WANT TO BE A GOOD WOMAN sings Cat Power, maybe that GOOD GIRL is the same girl as THE GIRL WITH THE MOST CAKE, Courtney Love says that and I believe her, if there's a day to be the girl with the biggest piece of cake surely it's on her birthday, the day of her twenty-ninth birthday, the last year, my last year, will be an ideal year, it'll be my year, that twenty-nine that I've dreaded for so long, at twenty-nine I'll eat cake every day, I'll write every day too, all the time, you'll see, I'll be Nelly, Marie-Sissi, Angie, Lizzie, a sorority of doomed women, I'll take on the voice of the women who knew to cry out before me, refrains that I know by heart to ground myself in the continuity of the expression of a suffering lived a thousand times over by people who aren't me.

---

3. Kat George, "Who Is Pop Music's 'Good Girl' and How the Hell Do We Get Rid of Her", *Noisey*, November 2 2015, https://noisey.vice.com/en_us/article/rmj5kn/who-is-pop-musics-goodgirl-and-how-the-hell-do-we-get-rid-of-her.

YOU MAY BE WONDERING: why thirty, why that number and not another? Obviously, you may assume that it's Nelly Arcan who put that idea in my head. After all, she talks openly about it in *Hysteric*, it's there in black and white, or black and yellow like the pages in my old copy. I got the idea long before that, though. As long as I can remember, I could never imagine a future for myself after turning thirty: thirty was the beginning of the end, the moment when you start to slip down a long slope and I wanted to escape from the descent, suddenly disappear, without goodbyes dripping with drama for this world that never understood me anyway. So it's been a long time, it was slowly forged in my mind, once again Elizabeth Wurtzel takes the words out of my mouth, or my mind, or my fingers, whatever: **IT HAPPENED GRADUALLY, THEN SUDDENLY**. Wurtzel is referring to depression, but I'm talking about aging. It's the same thing after all, or anyway, in this case, in my specific case, it happened gradually and then suddenly: I was young and I couldn't picture myself old, in my twenties when people would ask my age I'd always answer twenty-eight, they were credulous and I was credible, I mean, how can you tell someone's age, if she says so then it must be true, why would you make yourself older, normally you would round down when you lie, but to say that is not to know what it's like to be young and pretty, to think you have your whole life ahead of you, saying twenty-eight like saying infinity, saying thirty, a number that will never come and if it does I'll see it coming and I'll avoid it, like I once avoided a deer on the road, the deer was running in front of me, in front of my car, on my left there was the river, on my right there was the ditch. Montérégie is beautiful, instead of choosing one or the other it kept going straight ahead, in the light of my headlights, and then it ended up leaping into the ditch. I would have chosen the water, in fact every time I would take that route it would cross my mind, it would terrify me knowing that just a little turn of the steering wheel could send me straight into the river, just a moment of distraction, one day you're alive and the next you're not, that's it, **GRADUALLY THEN SUDDENLY**. Thirty, an even number, everyone knows odd numbers are ugly, an odd number implies that there's someone extra or someone was put aside, you see there's math behind thirty, an elementary school subject that I hated, but I chose thirty because it's the next even number after my favourite even number, twenty-eight. Two times four will always make eight, plus in elementary school I was always number 8 because my last name starts with D, just once I was number six and it made me angry, but I guess it could have been worse, I could have been number seven. Yes I know: seven is the lucky number, but you'd have to be a real idiot to think there's luck in an odd number. I would say twenty-eight just like that; it was the even number that was closest to thirty, but that didn't go over. The problem is that now I have gone over twenty-eight, it's there in the rear-view mirror, I wave my hand at it now that I'm in twenty-nine-year-old limbo, a number I hate, but not as much as I hate the thought of turning thirty. I've weighed the pros and cons of aging, I wanted to buy into the promise of happiness, but I'm too poor and besides fuck capitalism, even though I spend entire days saving items in virtual carts, I never check out, "Capitalism suggests we can buy happiness; liberalism posits happiness as an integral part of citizenship (at least in North America); and neoliberalism implies that happines is hyper-mobile and hyper-accessible if only we buy into it."[4] But what happens to the women who don't cough up the cash, not just the ones who are too busy paying off their student loans, but those who refuse, as a political choice, to pay even a dime for a concept that is fundamentally free, when is happiness, what is happiness, happiness is a tomorrow that never comes. Anyway, today and for the rest of the year to come, the number twenty-nine is there in front of me and I don't know what to think anymore, I've been looking at it for a long time, I thought it would leap to one side or the other, but no, it's really here, so it'll be up to me to move, to choose between the river and the ditch, unless I keep driving straight ahead, in ten years of driving I've never had an accident, never had a fender-bender, never had a blemish on my record, first-in-class, so it should be alright, at twenty-nine years old maybe I should just floor it, thirty will get here soon enough, gradually then suddenly.

---

4. Erin Wunker, *Notes from a Feminist Killjoy*, Toronto, Book*Hug, 2016, p. 44.

AUGUST

I'll ADMIT: I HAVEN'T WRITTEN MUCH THESE LAST FEW DAYS, but it's because I've been busy reading Marie-Sissi, it's because I've been busy being depressed, crushed by the weight of the last days of July, the worst month in the entire history of my life. July is ugly, awful, dripping with dreariness, the worst month for a birthday, because the nice romantic story is that I was destined to be born on July 31st, I should have been a Leo instead of a Cancer, I should have had a strong mane instead of a soft shell. If I had been born on July 31st I would have shared a birthday with Elizabeth Wurtzel who turned forty-eight yesterday, if I too had been born on July 31st we would have had an age difference of exactly nineteen years and we would both be Leos. If I were a Leo, maybe Elizabeth Wurtzel would reply to my Tweets, she would answer when

I tweet at her: "@ElizabethWurtzel OMG HAPPY BIRTHDAY LIZZIE WE SHARE THE SAME BIRTHDAY," we would share a birthday just like we share the same issues. By the way, speaking of issues: Marie-Sissi's second book really bugged me and I had to force myself to finish it, I'm good at forcing myself to read since I started studying literature, it's silly but it's true, basically it's about Emilie-Kiki who sleeps with her lit professor, she reminds us every two pages how much she loves this prof, it's almost a litany, a bit like Nelly, it's more of the same from a crazy girl who won't let go, and in this specific case she isn't letting go of dick from a lit prof who's dumb enough to have an extramarital affair with his twenty-seven-year-old student. Marie-Sissi tells us this story for a hundred and fifty pages at the end of which I shut the book while telling myself FUCK THIS. I listened to an audiobook instead, I listened to David Lynch tell me about transcendental meditation. When David finished talking to me, I realized it was after midnight, it was six minutes past midnight and it was then that I saw that Elizabeth Wurtzel had tweeted that it was her birthday, at 11:45

p.m. on July 31st it was Lizzie's birthday and since she tweeted it at the end of the day I was forced to wish her a happy belated birthday, which doesn't really matter, since Elizabeth Wurtzel never replies to my Tweets anyway. I lay down on my bed, ready to sleep tight and not let the bedbugs bite, thinking **WWDLD**, meaning **WHAT WOULD DAVID LYNCH DO**, and the obvious answer would be: **COOK QUINOA** like in the special bonus features of the *Inland Empire* DVD, so I got up to cook quinoa and while it simmered I told myself that August would be a wonderful month, it's a literary month and I've finished reading Marie-Sissi, I thought about David who says **YOU GOTTA HAVE FREEDOM TO HAVE TIME TO LET GOOD THINGS HAPPEN** and I simmered in my nocturnal freedom, I thought that once the quinoa had cooked I could focus on my freedom and let the month of August bring me good things, since I'm now a year older, I'm older than I was before.

I PROMISED MYSELF I'D WRITE EVERY DAY of this year number twenty-nine, but I shouldn't obsess about that. I know all about obsessions, but is it really a good idea to keep harping on about the same bad ideas? Therapists and moms would agree that negativity attracts negativity, obsessions bring on more obsessions, by the way I got a two-for-one in that department: my mom is a therapist, that's her profession, although for me she occupies the sole role of mother. It isn't like in the episode of *Radio Enfer* where Camille's therapist-mom asks her, "Camille, do you want to talk about it?" when Camille has a hard time opening the peanut butter jar, no, it's not like that, I'm not like that and my mom isn't like that either. I'm sure my mom would agree that it's a bad idea to let your blood boil, the problem is that I love that saying, I imagine hot blood burning through my veins, the only way to cool down would be to bleed out, but I guess the problem is that it would also kill me. So I need to live with that blood, the boiling kind, therapists and moms would agree that thinking you're a bad person is a sign of low self-esteem, that getting riled up thinking something bad is going to happen is a symptom of anxiety. Basically I'm a symptom of everything, but for what reasons exactly? I'd rather be Patricia Arquette in *Stigmata*: be clearly possessed, speak fifteen languages, make metro cars explode, and have it end as it should with an exorcism. At least if I were in *Stigmata* I'd be blonde and pretty, like Nelly, like Marie-Sissi and Lizzie too while we're at it, in short, I just wanted to say that you shouldn't obsess about things, you shouldn't get your blood pressure up, the torture is over for today, for this year, for this life. Have you seen the movie *Martyrs*? I auditioned to play the part of "the torture victim," yes, in quotes, because that's really the name of the role according to IMDB, in those days I would easily have accepted a nudity clause to have my body painted and to move my bones on screen, but whatever, I didn't get the part despite years of classical dance and learning the language of the body. I still saw the movie and I didn't sleep that night, a very good film, but *Martyrs* isn't real life, real life is being twenty-nine years old and trying not to obsess about anything, for that matter when I close my eyes, I see nothing, moms and therapists would agree that there's nothing better than visualization, so I close my eyes and I visualize nothing, not in the sense that I'm not visualizing, no, in the sense that I visualize the "nothing" itself. I look into the void, the void of my thirtieth birthday that approaches, I hear it tumbling down the stairs, slamming against the door to the lobby, it'll be up to me to open it, or not, I promised myself that I would write every day this year so I guess we'll see, I just need to stop obsessing, that's the key.

AT THIS POINT IN MY LITANY it would be fair to ask me who I write for, why I write, because after all, this isn't my LiveJournal from 2002, this isn't my MySpace from 2006, this isn't my Tumblr from 2008, no, this is my body which is given to you on paper, take it, read it, don't forget that if this heap of words is published posthumously it'll be because of Nelly, yes, Nelly who in *Hysteric* writes to her lover one last time, she knows he doesn't want her just like I know that life doesn't want me, I'm no one's lover if not my own, I love to dissect my flaws, explore the rifts from which my unhappiness trickles drip by drip, like champagne flowing from a cracked crystal glass, cracked just right, on the surface, lightly, but irredeemably broken. You'll find my words printed on paper, inked and anchored on the page, acidic bile that can't be erased even if you put all your effort into it, even if you put an entire life into it, even if you use a Mr. Clean magic eraser. No, I won't ever disappear from the page, even after disappearing from your lives, I'll always be there to remind you that, of course, everything passes, but nothing ever goes right, time goes by through new Netflix originals, on your screens Stella Gibson will still be wearing silk blouses, Joyce Byers will never untangle her hair, Piper Chapman won't stop being manipulative, it all goes on, and if ever it gets better with time I won't be there to see it, you can say that I gave up, that I abandoned ship, I ran away and left you to cry over my disappearance. You'll weep over my absence that you'll probably forget about quickly enough anyway, we have to stop believing that the dead take up all the room even if death itself is omnipresent in our lives, I swear to you that everyone who disappeared from existence will also disappear from your minds. It's inevitable, irreversible, I'm walking downhill on a long path, maybe I'll see you at the bottom, I'll call out to you to say that it feels good to be erased, that down here the days lose their lustre, the crystal fades, the cup overflows, bursts, explodes, the champagne spills all around and I bathe in it day after day, finally free from existence.

SEPTEMBER

I WAS NOT SHORTLISTED for the CBC prose prize, I don't see my piece or my face on the web page, but I did send them a photo, it was so pretty, I'm dressed in pink, my bangs are perfect, but no, I wasn't shortlisted and I need to say it out loud so that everyone knows that I'm not a winner, I have to shout it out to admit that I didn't use words like *cloistered* or *sanatorium*, I didn't talk about a sad childhood or a dead mother, I screwed up the recipe. I blame my creative writing professor, a Russian man who, instead of teaching us to win, droned on about **LEO TOLSTOY BEST RUSSIAN WRITER**, I blame my hands for failing my brain when it came time to write the winning words, I blame the number twenty-nine for arriving so quickly because unlike Liz Wurtzel I didn't have time to write a bestseller at twenty-seven, it's surprising, because when I was little

I won all the contests, I even won the Desjardins contest for the prettiest drawing, I swear: I won at everything, that's the tragedy of the child prodigy, **SHE WAS SO FULL OF PROMISE**. That's what Elizabeth Wurtzel says, one day you're full of promise and the next you don't win the Radio-Canada contest, that's how it is, you ask yourself how you got here, but you also remember: **GRADUALLY, THEN SUDDENLY**, those are Lizzie's words, **SLOWLY BUT SURELY** said the tortoise to the hare, when I was a kid I read fables before bed, not knowing that one day I'd be empty of promise, slowly but surely, I wasted it all. Slowly but surely I stopped believing that I'd ever do any good, besides I never believed in fairy tales because I don't like Prince Charmings, in Disney movies I only like Angelina Jolie because she accepts that she's the bad guy, **I'M THE VILLAIN BABY** she says in *Girl, Interrupted* in 1998, then in 2012 she takes the role of Maleficent, dressed all in black. By the way today I read in a scientific article that researchers discovered a colour that's blacker than black, a super black, so I told myself: **COOL THEY FOUND MY SOUL**, a black with no texture that absorbs everything and reflects nothing, that doesn't even reflect before it acts, just like I didn't reflect before sending a story to Radio-Canada, I didn't think about what a winning piece of writing would consist of, I just vomited my emotional bulimia onto the page. It's not that I was expecting glory, in fact, I didn't even expect to win, no, but I would really have liked for the quote to be about me for once: Marie is so **FULL OF PROMISE**, Marie, **SLOWLY BUT SURELY**, will become the **BEST CANADIAN WRITER**.

Château Marmont

Angelina Jolie
Actrice

Angelina Jolie, née Angelina Jolie Voight le 4 juin 1975 à Los Angeles, est une actrice, réalisatrice, scénariste, productrice, mannequin, philanthrope, écrivaine et ambassadrice de bonne volonté américano-cambodgienne. Wikipédia

Date et lieu de naissance : 4 juin 1975 (Âge: 42 ans), Los Angeles, Californie, États-Unis

Taille : 1,69 m

Enfants : Shiloh Jolie-Pitt, Maddox Jolie-Pitt, PLUS

Parents : Jon Voight, Marcheline Bertrand

Époux : Brad Pitt (m. 2014), Billy Bob Thornton (m. 2000–2003), Jonny Lee Miller (m. 1996–1999)

THERE'S SOMETHING I FORGOT TO MENTION when I talked about my love for Angelina Jolie: it's that I have a little Angelina in me, because Angelina is my middle name. It's written right there on my birth certificate, after my maternal grandmother whose name was also Angelina. I saw Angelina Jolie on screen for the first time in *Girl, Interrupted*, I was fourteen and that same night I wrote about her in my diary, in retrospect I think Angelina Jolie was my first celebrity crush. Yes, of course, first there was Ariel from *The Little Mermaid*, but that doesn't really count. In elementary school, my friends had covered their walls with giant posters of Devon Sawa or Leonardo DiCaprio, but they never really did it for me, probably because I was quietly waiting for Angie, you might say that it was worth the wait, I mean, once I laid eyes on Angelina Jolie's face nothing else mattered to me. I mean, Angelina Jolie as Lisa Rowe is all Hollywood needed, it's all I needed, by the way in my diary from back then you'll find a list of dreams I wanted to accomplish and one of them was "go to Hollywood to convince Angelina Jolie to dye her hair blonde again," because after *Girl, Inter-*

rupted she dyed her hair black again and in those days I wasn't goth enough to like that, I couldn't rid myself of the image of Lisa and her yellow hair, no, I wasn't yet able to see beauty in darkness, which in retrospect was probably a good thing. But there you have it, in 2001, after *Girl, Interrupted*, Angelina Jolie sort of fell into oblivion for me, which is sacrilege, I know, but between you and me, her movie *Tomb Raider* was for boys and I'm a girl, a girl who likes girls and girly things, chick flicks, in my girly Hollywood and my girly life there are only tragedies. Recently, my love for Angie came back in full swing, an obsession that's impossible to ignore, constant, ever-present like Maleficent's cheeks on Angie's face, yes, I think it's Maleficent who's to blame here, it's strange because in *Girl, Interrupted* Angie says **I'M PLAYING THE VILLAIN BABY, JUST LIKE YOU WANT**, and that's exactly what she does in *Maleficent*, fifteen years later she's still playing the bad guy. Because I love tragedy and villainy, I'm on Maleficent's site, the dark side, the stronger side, *Maleficent* revived my obsession with Angeline Jolie and ever since I've been spending my time answering the question **WWAD, WHAT WOULD ANGIE DO**, I try as much as possible to act in a way that would make Angie proud, it's important because if it were up to me, my motivation level would be in free-fall, I know myself, I need reasons to live, it doesn't matter what they are, I need scripts. When I was in seventh grade, I would play a game to motivate myself to go to school: I would imagine that I was being watched by an imaginary higher power, I would tell myself that if my actions were being monitored that would mean that I wasn't allowed to make mistakes, that was how I learned to be perfect, that's how I learned to colour-code the books in my locker and organize them by size. I needed motivation to live day by day, no need to believe in any sort of god, just a need to think of being watched, I don't know by who or by what, but it worked for me to feel like I met the standards of an imaginary person. Even today I keep playing that game, doing things for someone other than myself who would justify my actions. I'm not afraid, I know that if I don't find anyone there will always be Angie, and these days it's Angie because nothing else can compare. I was thinking about it yesterday when I was listening to Joan Baez and I told myself maybe it's time to give up, maybe it's time to do things only for myself. If that's the case, if that's the right decision, I'll need to say goodbye to Angie and I could let Joan Baez do it for me when she sings FAREWELL ANGELINA. If it doesn't work, if I don't forget about Angie, I can always console myself by returning to her, I can tell myself that this isn't the end of the obsession, because after all, when Joan Baez sings FAREWELL ANGELINA, she also sings I'LL SEE YOU IN A WHILE.

OCTOBER

I WONDER what Elizabeth Wurtzel is doing today. While I'm at it, I wonder what Angelina Jolie is doing today. Basically, I wonder what's happening outside of me because on my end, here and now, there isn't much happening, it's raining and I'm procrastinating, I don't live in L.A. or New York, from the comfort of my living room I tweet @ElizabethWurtzel and she doesn't reply, that's how it always is. I wonder what Lizzie is doing, I wonder if she's sober, because today I want to confess to Elizabeth Wurtzel that I had three beers last night, I broke the rule of sobriety, **IT'S THE FIRST DRINK THAT GETS YOU DRUNK** Eileen Myles told me, yes I met Eileen Myles. Instead of talking about poetry we talked about sobriety, but Eileen Myles didn't know who Elizabeth Wurtzel was, even though they both live in New York, it's strange, they're both also literary rock stars: Elizabeth Wurtzel published her first novel at twenty-seven, a novel that became an instant bestseller, while Eileen Myles was becoming the idol of young girls like me who aspire to write the real, the tangible that bursts when we throw ourselves into it. At that time, I wasn't publishing anything and I wasn't becoming anything, it was the nineties and I was only ten years old. Then, later on, when I turned twenty-seven myself, I didn't publish a bestseller, but I stopped drinking, I stopped drinking the week the *Daily Mail* published a video of Angie apparently on drugs with her so-called dealer, revealing her so-called dark past, although if people had paid attention they would understand that her past wasn't dark—it was lit by cameras all over the place, it's very simple, there's an interview where Angie says **I KNOW ADDICTION IN ALL FORMS** and she's very serious, she squints her eyes a little and that means it's true, I know because I know her face well. Ex-junkies wonder until when their past will haunt them, Natasha Lyonne said that, how a junkie stays a junkie. Maybe Cat Marnell needs to be asked that question, another literary New

Yorker who falls into the category of beautiful survivors, but I won't ask because I'm too scared of her, because once I tweeted @CatMarnell that she was like @ElizabethWurtzel and she replied **YES OF COURSE DUMBASS BECAUSE ALL JUNKIES ARE THE SAME**, but that wasn't what I was trying to insinuate, I should have just kept my mouth shut, except I'm not good at keeping things inside, it's like the joke: **HOW CAN YOU TELL A JUNKIE IS LYING? HER LIPS ARE MOVING.** It wasn't Cat or Angie or Lizzie who said that, it was Gia Carangi's mother, and if we can trust anyone's word it's definitely hers, I mean, her daughter died of AIDS contracted from a used needle, so we won't challenge her on that, for that matter my lips too are constantly moving, I'm in the same boat, I lie all the time, I complain, I don't stop because "We must stay unhappy with this world,"[5] I refuse to sit and contemplate the scenery that's never pretty enough to be looked at anyway. Of course I could lie, yes, tell you **EVERYTHING'S GREAT**, *ça va bien* like the song by Kathleen, but it would

---

5. Sara Ahmed, *The Promise of Happiness*, Durham, Duke University Press, 2010, p. 105.

sound fake. Eileen Myles told me I was a liar because in a poem I wrote for her workshop I used the lie as a literary device, I mentioned my brothers and sisters even though I'm an only child, a liar unmasked, shy, with my lips always moving, but I haven't ever given an interview, I never went on *Tout le monde en parle* to avenge Nelly for how he treated her and spit my wine into Guy's face, I never went on *Oprah* to ask Lizzie to reply to my tweets, I never went on *Saturday Night Live* to sing a song in which I publicly apologize to Cat Marnell. In terms of public speaking, all I've done are those church basement meetings where you confess your sins, I guess I could go back to them actually, at least those people will listen to me, they'll watch my lips move.

HERE'S ONE THING THAT'S TRUE: I swear that at any given moment, I'm thinking about forgetting, escaping, drinking. While for me that's a confession, for you it's nothing but entertainment, you read my secrets with your eyes big and round like the chips they hand out in those basements or other places that are hard to find from the street. I know I'm not alone, that there's nothing exceptional about my story: after all, I've seen the others, the women who meet up in the churches and community centres, I know them all, even the ones who will never set foot inside, **AN ADDICT IS AN ADDICT IS AN ADDICT**, Gertrude Stein would say, may as well put them all in the same basket, because even if drug addiction has many faces, at the end of the day it's all the same: panicking because you can't find your lighter your pipe your paper your baggie your straw your spoon your needle, running to the dep because it's 11:00 p.m. and it's going to close or because it's 8 a.m. and it just opened, seducing your dealer to front you a quarter, a three and a half, an eightball. So predictable, so manipulative, that's what they say about us and our act, we play not just with our life but with your gullibility, I'm really sorry, but I can't stop. I'm talking about my unhealthy obsessions and you'll say, "Why talk about it then," and I answer simply, "Why not?" Why not document the time that goes by, that never goes well, the minutes that accumulate while each one is a feat, a little victory that I lean over like it's the cradle of a newborn, I scrutinize myself constantly, years of therapy to learn to measure the almost nonexistent progress of the part of me that always wants more and for which nothing is ever "enough." It started when I was eight, when, fascinated by the idea of smoking, I wanted to steal some cigarettes, bum a puff, a smoke, some nausea. So I did what any semi-sane child would do, I took a cinnamon stick and struck a match, I let the spiced smoke into my lungs. With my wrist bent, my index and middle fingers nice and straight, my mouth closing, pinched, a real Audrey Hepburn from a cheap poster bought at Rif-Raf at the Promenades St-Bruno mall, looking dejected realizing that's all that smoking is. Already at that age, smoking wasn't enough, I was looking for something unattainable, but I didn't know what yet, so

I decided to move onto the next step, I went into the pantry to find some dry herbs to roll up and, not having any idea what kind of paper to use, I took a piece of paper from the printer to cut a rectangle out of with my blue right-handed scissors, with the initials MD on the blade. I placed the herbs right in the middle and rolled the paper up as best I could, praying that no one would walk into my room. They say that for addicts the ritual is as important as the consumption itself, the heart racing and the anticipation of knowing we'll find a familiar rush. Already as a child I was throwing myself headfirst into a trap so carefully laid, barbecue lighter in hand I wandered around the back yard looking for a dark corner where I could light my creation, I had no idea that what I was going to be inhaling was black, acrid smoke. Anyway, it didn't matter to me, because all I wanted to accomplish with this rebellious gesture was to escape from myself for just a moment, fail in my role of head of the class, yes, after all, this is a story like any other where the protagonist inherits a nickname fit for a sub-category of movies on Netflix: **POOR LITTLE RICH GIRL.**

It continued in a suburban bungalow where I took my first sip of alcohol, while already at thirteen my friends were doing mescaline at the top of mount Saint-Hilaire and ending up in an after school special, I was the token scaredy cat, the one who would warn everyone when the cops were coming, the one who would call the parents, the one who made sure no one choked on vomit, what shocking behaviour, maybe I wanted to protect myself from myself, that was all before I gave in completely, falling into the exaggeration of nighttime escapades, the lies hidden in a light pink dresser drawer, the calls in hushed voices to discuss plans that were hidden from parents. I finally tasted it all at once, mint-flavoured liqueur on the lips of boys, rum & cokes on the lips of girls, it was like a barricade had blown up and the nice girl turned into a demon, one who makes up stories to tell her family, one who scribbles in her agenda while her French teacher yells at her, one who starts hanging out with Chloe whose dad is a dealer, Chloe and her little plastic bags that smelled like skunk, Chloe and her Discman that we used to listen to hip-hop with on the sidewalk, runs to the dep that sells fried chicken legs owned by a guy named Shithead. Shithead would supply us with loose cigarettes and we'd sprinkle the tobacco into our pipe, we would watch the city get blurry before our eyes and then say, "Those two street lights are really straight," and then go to school, to math class where I couldn't understand a thing, but where I'd still get near-perfect grades. The cruel magic trick of life is to make nice girls believe that nothing bad will ever happen to them and that they're above it all, because that way they can sink while maintaining their innocence. Contrary to what you may believe, it didn't start the day I drank so much sangria in a poetry workshop at Concordia that I had to call my dealer to meet up with him on Bishop Street before locking myself in the bathroom at Reggies (R.I.P.), I said yes to consumption, **GO ASK ALICE** and she said yes, so I dove in and that's when I started forgetting. Forgetting the toilets, the ceilings, the walls, the apartments, the multiple after-hours spots where we made new best friends in front of the bathroom mirror, no longer even bothering to avert our eyes when one of us went to piss in the toilet in the corner of the room. If all the places where I drank and used were to light up on a map of Montreal, there'd be a High Lights Festival big enough for the most beautiful Loto-Quebec-sponsored fireworks, because in fact, in those days, the whole city was on fire and I would let myself burn on the cross at the top of Mount Royal like I was in a Madonna video, I would let myself burn from all ends, every orifice, every crack, the fire would fill the void and the void would put out the fire, **REPEAT, ONCE AGAIN, WITHOUT FEELING**. It starts over every day of my life when I look at the clock and tell myself **JUST ONE MORE MINUTE**, I try to put off the hour of my destruction, push the limits, but we have to consider that healing is an illusion, **ADDICTION IS A DISEASE** they say, but not really, not if you never heal from it, once an addict always an addict, my substance problem is due not just to genetics but also several social factors, so how do you fully heal, how do you bounce back in a society that is constantly knocking you down when you're born with a soft shell, I have thin skin, I'm a Cancer. **JUST ONE MORE MINUTE**, just a tiny mountainous effort, I tell myself that with experience it gets easier, I give myself a pep talk fit for a sobriety champion, I repeat the words I've heard a thousand times that magically work one morning, **IT WORKS IF YOU WORK IT**, like magic! Magic like when I was a kid and I would concoct potions in my parents' backyard, a little mud, a little grass, lots of time spent coming up with these witchy recipes, once a witch always a witch, so I've been an expert for a while now in liquids, pills, powders, an entire life spent calculating, waiting, suffering, smiling, mixing up properly, only to realize in the end that it's a constant state for me, every hour, every minute, every second: it starts over, **JUST ONE MORE MINUTE**.

NOVEMBER

T00 INTENSE. That's what they whisper in the aisles of the Salon du Livre where I scream your name, I scream Nelly, Nelly, I ask what time this author will have her book signing as I point at your book and everyone smiles from the corner of their mouth, out of the corner of their eye they see me take a selfie in front of the Éditions du Seuil booth, it's obvious that you've left without a trace, just like it's obvious that I'm crazy, a *Hysteric* like you. Some are horrified by my question, by my violation of the sacrosanct code that prohibits invoking the dead, but to them I say **MY FAVOURITE AUTHORS ARE ALL DEAD OR DEPRESSED**, that's my excuse for wandering around under the neon lights that are my own projectors, I barely come up to your ankles and I know it, I'm only five foot four, I've got nothing on these great women who left their mark before me on the rough carpet of the Place Bonaventure convention centre, my secret is that I have only one reason for being here: to put on a show, the show of my love for you, grandiose, pathetic, if I could get you to sign my copy of *Hysteric*, I'd have you sign all the books that I own as well, my entire library, whether they're your works or not, it doesn't matter. On that note, here's a confession: I left a kiss somewhere in the pages of one of your books, in a copy that a stranger will buy and I hope they smile at the pink outline of my lips, at this proof of boundless love. In the middle of the afternoon I saw a kid roll around on the floor in front of the red Flammarion stand and I thought I saw myself, my spirit animal, a me making a scene, crying over your disappearance, wailing over the pain caused by the emptiness in my heart. I wander from booth to booth, I give hugs, I smile, I buy things, my lips move on their own while my head is elsewhere, far away, in the bathroom where I do a key bump while nobody notices, no one would believe that good girls want to evaporate, try to forget, numb themselves. The last time I set foot in here was in 2009, I was working for a big pig, a paunchy editor who slept with all his prey, while he was on the prowl I would take naps in the closet, among all the coats I would close my eyes to disappear for a moment, to forget the parties from the night before where everyone was openly making out. All the big and small spaces are interconnected, there are no secrets anymore when everyone is patting each other on the back. I wish this masquerade would end, I wish we'd make a date through Messenger, I wish we'd give each other a cue to go make out in the bathroom, I love the marble and gold that adorn the stalls, I imagine myself putting my mouth on your breasts as you sigh, I imagine us giving in to the magic of the present moment or some other line worthy of an esoteric personal growth book, the truth is that I don't know how to grow, all I want is to remain in my pathos. **I'M ONLY HAPPY WHEN IT RAINS** Shirley Manson sings, I'm only happy when it's drizzling darkness, that's where I belong, seated comfortably between two or three lovers that don't really want me— **POUR YOUR MISERY DOWN ON ME**, go on, I can take it. Having an expiry date gives me the courage to keep wading through misery, it's my little magic trick, when I reach that long awaited number, thirty, I will be gone without leaving a trace, and you'll all shrug and say: **SHE WAS TOO INTENSE.**

I'VE NEVER READ HUBERT AQUIN, I'VE ONLY READ NELLY ARCAN, that's what I say when I want to think of myself as good, I say it and repeat it like a refrain, like a litany, like a Nelly fleeing to France from Quebec, fleeing the colony to conquer the king, the queen, and all their subjects. Only I don't seduce anyone with my pseudo-healthy confessions, my literary admissions, I'm not seducing anyone when I stay on my couch with my coffee reading *Je veux une maison faite de sorties de secours*, yes it's true, that's what I want, my open-air home, my house made for a writer who hides from the outside world, from the hail, from the snow, from the minus thirty weather, I hide with Nelly and we read we read we read like larvae soaked in lattes, I'm a literary larva stuffing herself with the words she didn't know how to write, reading the words of strangers who cry over the disappearance of the great novelist who took her own life. Of course, I hate when people call her Nelly even though I do it myself, I prefer Arcan like the greats, I like her better than all the others, but anyway, since Nelly rhymes with Lizzie, with Marie-Sissi, with Angie, it'll be for the cause, this noble cause of weeping over the one we lost, to write an obituary of her literary life. We all dream of writing the novel, of writing the TV show, of writing the movie called *Nelly*, I'm not any better than those who take a "piece of the corpse to revel in the genius,"[6] I'm fleeing my thirties through words because "Women need to avoid their thirties, where their demise begins sooner,"[7] so I write I write I write out my life in order to move from object to subject, a controlled transformation in which magic is an illusion. Even if we repeat the magic words three times, even if we read it backwards, I write from A to Z and from one to thirty to lay out on paper the blankness of my life, the sickly paleness of my character traits, my fear of aging that starts with an M, M like Marie, M like morbidity, M like when Bruno Pelletier sings about love in his song *AIME*, love as a cure-all, loving in order to be

---

6. Martine Delvaux, "La robe de Nelly Arcan", in Claudia Larochelle (dir.), *Je veux une maison faite de sorties de secours : réflexions sur la vie et l'œuvrel'oeuvre de Nelly Arcan*, Montréal, VLB, 2015, p. 127, free translation.

7. Carl Leblanc, "Caniches roses, pâtes infectésinfectes et blagues pornos", in Claudia Larochelle (dir.), *Je veux une maison faite de sorties de secours : réflexions sur la vie et l'œuvrel'oeuvre de Nelly Arcan*, Montréal, VLB, 2015, p. 115, free translation.

saved, by the way I have a date tonight, a date in the soft light of a bar where we'll trace our blurry contours with our confessions because it's through confession that we find salvation. It's through confession that the other person's shape is revealed, the shape of their chest, their mouth, their nose, their ass, the shape of our existence, what I'm trying to say is that tonight I'll lay out my secrets in the dark and all that'll be seen in them is fire, the glimmer of the candles that blurs the shadows of truth, because just as where there's smoke there's fire, where there are confessions there are lies.

IT'S SATURDAY, it's two in the morning and I'm wondering if Fiona Apple is happy. I'm watching recent concerts, she's *tiny tiny tiny* and people are commenting **OMG SHE DIDN'T AGE WELL** and I wonder if it's possible to age in peace, just age; not well, not badly, I wonder if it's possible to simply continue to live, one day at a time like the song my grandmother would sing to me before going to church on Sunday mornings. People are writing **I WONDER IF SHE'S ON DRUGS** because people who don't understand persistent suffering need this obsession with finding a concrete, tangible, material reason. Women have to stay young and pretty or they have to free themselves from their suffering by aging, as if age is a guarantee of happiness, aging like a Club Med retirement where all the snowbirds are shaking hands. No one likes to see women sink into sadness or stay depressed, once unhappy always unhappy, Celine said it and I'll say it again: **WE NEVER CHANGE**. It reminds me of that interview where they ask Angelina Jolie **DO YOU MISS BEING A BAD GIRL** and Angie smiles, quietly, she squints, she bursts out laughing, then she says **I'M STILL A BAD**

GIRL, she never stopped being one, it isn't because you stopped watching her that she transformed into a good girl. It's Saturday, it's two in the morning and five hours ago I watched a cat die in the street, its eyes were bulging, it was hit by a car, I was petrified, the SPCA brought it to Laval to put it down and I was screaming TAKE ME TO LAVAL, TAKE ME TO LA RONDE, La Ronde where I'll be able to get dizzy before dying myself. Five hours later I haven't forgotten any of it, time goes by, but nothing happens, nothing goes well, not even writing, I wish I could just slip away even though I should be telling you the truth. Here's how things go for big girls, I wasn't the one who established it, Wurtzel said it: the first novel is about depression, the second novel is about addiction. The goal is to never be sober, to be overwhelmed by the concrete and the abstract. I do plan to try to fulfill my mission on earth, my fate, a concept as empty for me as a Julia Roberts romcom, all I want to do is fill the void, because I've seen it all, I was schooled by the screen, a human billboard who needs to base her life on what she's been shown, my life is yours, take it and look at it, I've been nourished by movies where the women are young, nice, and pretty before they become old, mean, and ugly, time takes its toll like a curse, I've told you and I'll tell you again, I'm the villain, the bad guy, I own it, it allows me to reassure myself about the future, it helps separate me from the masses, I'm looking you in the eye and I'm telling you **I WILL NEVER AGE WELL.**

DECEMBER

I TALKED A LOT TODAY, I didn't stop for even a second, my lips moved all day long, it's simple, anyone could learn all my secrets if they stayed with me long enough, the truth is that I have no secrets, because I'd rather say everything, unpack everything, expose everything even if it makes me vulnerable, that's my radical softness tactic, "radical softness is the idea that unapologetically sharing your emotions is a political move and a way to combat the societal idea that feelings are a sign of weakness."[8] To protect myself, I'd like to have a sign on my forehead that says **FRAGILE**, like what Elizabeth Wurtzel describes in *Prozac Nation*, once again I'm not original because Lizzie has already said it all, I'd like to wear my **FRAGILE** sign so people aren't mistaken: even if I say everything, all at once, I'm definitely crazy.

---

8. Meg Zulch, "Lora Mathis," *Hooligan Magazine*, no. 11, September 2015, https://issuu.com/hooliganmag/docs/issue_11.

Speaking of crazy: in *Girl, Interrupted*, when Winona Ryder asks **BUT WHAT DO YOU DO IF YOU DON'T HAVE ANY SECRETS**, Angie answers **THEN YOU'RE A LIFER LIKE ME**. Angie says that because she has no secrets to reveal in therapy so she's doomed to be crazy for the rest of her life, of course there's a difference between not having secrets in the sense of telling people everything and not having secrets in the sense of having nothing to hide, in my case it's both, all of the above, it's mostly that I throw my words into people's faces to see if they'll buckle under the weight of my confessions or if they'll be strong enough to keep listening, like emotional Olympic events where only the strongest win, only sensitive ears can get to the end, in truth, up to now people have done okay, hard to say if it's because they're solid or just curious, perverse, intrigued, entertained; whatever it is, because I'm a bit of an actress and I'm performing my own words, the more I play the part the more I detach myself from my secrets, which is certainly a good thing, a good girl—out of the characters in *Girl, Interrupted* I'm more Susanna than Lisa, sadly once again I'm not and will never be Angelina Jolie, physically I look more like Winona Ryder, it's true. While I'm talking, I tell myself that I'm saving the ink I'd use in my diary and that's a good thing because ink and paper have a price whereas words don't cost a thing, maybe just a little modesty, it doesn't cost me much of it for me to talk that way. "You call it oversharing. I call it a life instinct."[9] It's a small price to pay since I'm an exhibitionist by nature: it must be the ballet classes, it must be the theatre classes, it must the whatever classes that made it so I'd rather perform than hide, I should have auditioned for theatre schools, that's what I always said. The more I perform, anyway, everything becomes less serious, which is a good thing because I need to smile and laugh so that my mouth can be occupied with anything other than spitting out all these words. Mouths are made for smiling too and even if I don't have Angelina's mouth I'll still try to make it happen, smile a little and grit my teeth so I can shut up just long enough to forget how to speak, just long enough to keep silent, a silence labelled **FRAGILE**.

---

[9]. Cat Marnell, "On the Death of Whitney Houston: Why I Won't Ever Shut Up about My Drug Use," *xoJane*, February 13 2012, https://www.xojane.com/entertainment/whitney-houston-dead.

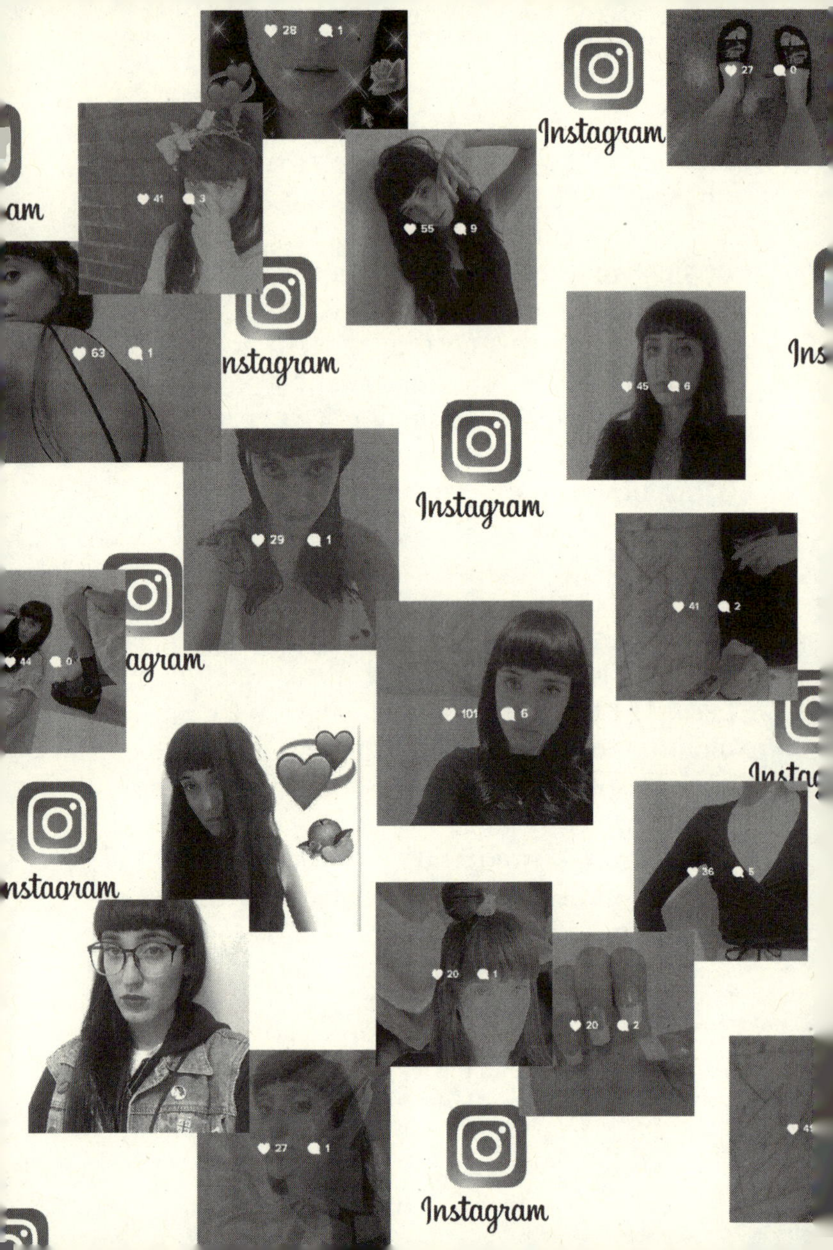
Instagram
Instagram
Instagram
Instagram

OF COURSE I KNOW that it wasn't really a good idea to go spend Christmas alone in Las Vegas, but all I wanted to do was leave, erase myself, escape from the holiday cheer that only reminds me that for other people this time means happiness and joy, Facebook family photos, conversations around the coffee machine about the exploits of their youngest, Instagram posts of vacations at the cottage by the lake, yes, all of that happens in other people's lives while it never happens for me, things never go well no matter what I do, so may as well spend all my money on a trip that will let me believe for a moment that I'm a character in a self-help book. **CHANGE YOUR LIFE IN ONE EASY TRIP**, I spend my money on Expedia with my Visa while others buy gifts at the Eaton Centre, once again everything revolves around me, in the self-help section I'm far from a bestseller, I'm more like a heroine from a Joan Didion novel, **I AM WHAT I AM AND TO LOOK FOR REASONS IS BESIDE THE POINT** Maria Wyeth says in *Play It as It Lays*, Maria driving in the desert, on the road to ruin beneath the palm trees, as for me I'm running till I'm out of breath through the red and green decorations that adorn the Strip that's lit up all year round, the pink flamingos of the Flamingo Hotel wearing little elf hats. I pretend to be interested in them as I smoke my menthol Marlboros, even though I'm not even a smoker, I came here to pretend I'm someone else, build myself a life far from the eyes of those who know me, dare to forget my troubles for a few days—but it never works. It doesn't work when I spend all day walking for miles all the way to the In-N-Out burger just behind the New York-New York Hotel; it doesn't work when I buy rose-scented bath bombs at Lush for the beige-coloured bathtub of my hotel room where I drink glass after glass of white wine; it doesn't work when I go out in a mini-skirt in the Nevada cold with my giant alcoholic slushie in hand; it doesn't work when I drink a fifteen-dollar martini while fixated on a Dolly Parton-themed slot machine; it doesn't work when in Old Vegas I pretend to be a food blogger to get as many free shrimp cocktails as I can; it doesn't work when at the reception I stand on one foot then the other and look at the ground mumbling **MY LOVER WILL PROBABLY JOIN ME LATER**

TONIGHT; it especially doesn't work when, on the flight back, a young couple tells me **WE JUST GOT MARRIED**, they confess to me starry-eyed, they ask if I went to Vegas alone, I don't feel like answering yes, I just say **I WENT TO MEET SOME FRIENDS**. People think I'm brave for travelling alone, but you have to understand: it isn't out of courage or recklessness or passion that I'm doing it, it's out of despair and torture and discouragement. I'm travelling to try to join my imaginary friends like Maria Wyeth, friends that don't feel any more optimism toward life than I do, I'm travelling to San Francisco for Michelle Tea, I'm travelling to New York for Elizabeth Wurtzel, I'm travelling to Boston for Sylvia Plath, I'm travelling to chase down the literary idols who are my sisters, my friends, my lovers, my mothers, my muses, the only ones who really understand me, who know why I want to erase myself so badly before the unsettling spectre of my thirtieth birthday.

JANUARY

I MAKE A SAD FACE when I rest my chin on my hand to stare at my computer screen, I'm staring at my MacBook where I'm reading that suicides are more prevalent among people who appear to have a great life, a great life meaning an Instagram account with plates that are full but not too full, a great life means family photos with kids smiling just the right amount, people who appear to be happy while I ask "What does happiness do?"[10] When people ask my age I can't say "twenty-eight, finally," no, I have to say "twenty-nine, just twenty-nine" and then they'll talk to me about entering my thirties, I've got my chin in my hand and my face in a frown while I read that in their thirties people become more empathetic because it usually means they've lived through a few dramatic events, the loss of their grandmother, an abortion, a divorce, a breakup, in short, people have

---

10. Sara Ahmed, *op. cit.*, p. 2.

gone through their own personal tragedies, which makes them more sensitive to other people's tragedies, so there's hope in the future and I see hope at the bottom of the glasses of wine I drink in the winter cold. We drink slower but we drink till the last drop, we call that the wisdom that comes with age, I finish the last drops of all the glasses, all the bottles, I'm here to absorb other people's tragedies, to fill myself with other people's feelings, functioning through happiness by proxy because personally I don't feel anything other than the weight of my own sad face. Gravity pulls on my eyelashes and snatches a few tears down with it, yes, I'm building myself a boat to learn to surf the wave, I hold back my tears by holding onto my chin to measure the earthquake in my face, I review the extent of the damage by counting the barely-concealed fine lines, I'm starting to show signs of age, I'm starting to get wrinkles, my wisdom hides in the bags under my eyes and sometimes when I rest my chin on my hand I softly sigh and say "Twenty-nine, now," and in the cup of my hand I collect just enough salt water to baptize myself, to wish myself a happy new year.

EVERY DAY is someone's birthday or the anniversary of something and every day I just walk by, no I will not wish you a happy birthday on your voicemail or your wall, you could say that it's because all that matters is me me me, but that theory seems incorrect because this month I missed my very own half-birthday, the first of January—yes, my half-birthday falls exactly on New Year's Day, a double burden, the pressure of being at the half-way point of my thirtieth year combined with resolutions about going to the gym, to therapy, to physio, to a life coach, on January first I've passed the half-way point of this infamous year when everything will eventually pass while nothing actually happens. Nothing happens in January because it's the graveyard of the year and I always think about the ice storm of 1998, I think about my *Much Dance 97* cassette and I sing IT'S A BEAUTIFUL LIFE WOH-OH-OH-OH as I watch the branches fall onto the roofs of cars, as I watch my shoulders hunch under the weight of my own problems, at the cost of sixty-five dollars per physiotherapy session half-covered by the UQAM student insurance plan, I do my exercises pulling on the yellow band and hoping that a straight back is the promise of a better future, but I know that not everything is uphill, why fixate on your posture when everything else is crooked, I don't know, but because I'm a perfectionist I'll fixate on my bones till I'm a corpse, I have experience, until I was twenty-two I weighed less than a hundred pounds. Katie Holmes weighs a hundred and six pounds, I saw it on the cover of *Us Weekly*, I wonder how much Angelina Jolie weighs, I fixate on the details of the present because I'm rotting long-term. I remember useless things like your date of birth and your zodiac sign, I'll even remember your rising sign that you explained to me five minutes ago with your wine glass in hand, it's true that Cancers are self-centred, focused on their useless little feelings, "Our culture is quick to dismiss the emotional as illegitimate, insubstantial, not worth considering [...] but by refusing the connection between mind and body, we neglect an important area of research and also accept the misogynistic and foolish tradition of regarding a subset of 'female' pain as non-existent, exaggerated, imaginary, a sign of weakness."[11] I give up, I'm just waiting to see you brandishing that *Sextrology* book to see if we're compatible, it would be nice to spend the month of January with someone, as if it were the beginning of something beautiful even if technically it's the beginning of the end, the beginning of the second half of my thirtieth year, Cancer against Capricorn, two opposite signs, emotion and reason, what does it mean, it means ultimately I'll be doomed to keep moving toward the illusion of improvement, IT'S A BEAUTIFUL LIFE WOH-OH-OH-OH, I WOULD LIKE TO SPEND IT WITH YOU or at least just the month of January, just long enough to see if the *Sextrology* book is true, just long enough for me to forget the passing of time, just long enough for you to realize I'm just as DUMB as Brigitte Fontaine is CONNE.

---

11. Amy Berkowitz, *Tender Points*, Oakland, Timeless, Infinite Light, 2015, p. 92.

FEBRUARY

Here's a lie: Life at twenty-nine goes by smoothly, no matter what I do or don't do, whether I want to or not, whether I contemplate my good moves or my bad ones, time passes and flows like water under a bridge, like water off a duck's back, or whatever other metaphor that's as peaceful as a lake in the summer. Lies aside, here's the truth: life happens like the Ice Bucket Challenge dunked on your head by surprise, like the thin layer of ice on the lake that breaks under the weight of a drunk uncle who's too adventurous, like a torrent of slushie from the depanneur flowing from a broken machine, life happens with misery and crashes and blows, because already these few months I've lived under the reign of the number twenty-nine have left me shaken. I come up with beginnings of sentences in my head while I'm taking a shower, because it's in the shower that inspiration strikes. It's not original, but it's true, in the shower I think of the opening sentences and as soon as I step onto my bath mat the words are erased. Then I eat salads, I fold clothes, I put on dresses, I forget to write down my vague memory of the words that I'm sure would be much better on the page than down the shower drain, but that's how it is, I have bad short-term memory and I'm a Cancer, a water sign who takes pleasure in the ever-shifting imagery of sadness, who buys waterproof mascara to review it on Châtelaine **WOULD RECOMMEND, MUCH RESISTANT TO TEARS**, who nods her head when Jojo Savard says **THE MOON WILL BRING EXTRA SPECIAL GOOD VIBES TO CANCER**, I approve, the same way I nod along when I read Lizzie who says **I KNOW THAT I'M STARTING TO DRIVE PEOPLE CRAZY**, I know that I'm a "wound-dweller,"[12] when Lizzie talks about alienating herself from everyone who loves her even the slightest bit, she's talking about the time she spent in Florida, isolated from her life in the West Village, yes,

---

12. Leslie Jamison, *The Empathy Exams*, Minneapolis, Graywolf Press, 2014, p. 186.

our Lizzie was in Florida obsessing over the death penalty, she was obsessing over details, she was studying big law books to memorize everything in case of an eventual debate with condo neighbours or the cashier at 7-Eleven, yes, Lizzie was already showing an aptitude for legal texts, foreshadowing, since later in life, once she was sober, Lizzie pursued legal studies at Yale, no less, apparently all those nights she spent pulverizing her brain with clumsily ground up Ritalin didn't hurt her all that much, apparently everything we accomplish, good or bad, ends up coming in handy sooner or later, so tell me, Doctor how will my mascara and my Youtube astrology videos come in handy, will they help me become an expert in the archiving of sadness with a crumpled map of the stars as a background, I'll read the cotton candy pink Cancer horoscope and tell them: "**LIZZIE WURTZEL WILL BRING YOU EXTRA SPECIAL GOOD VIBES**, throw your ideas out with the bath water and don't forget that mascara is on sale this week at Jean Coutu."

I JUST FINISHED MY REREAD OF *MORE NOW AGAIN*, Lizzie's second book, and it hit me, I almost fell over in the shower, the shower where all my ideas come and go, in the shower I thought: I remember very clearly having read an interview with Wurtzel where the journalist mentions that Lizzie is drinking a glass of wine at their meeting spot in New York or more precisely the West Village, Lizzie is drinking a very light rosé, a blend with a pink and white checkered taste tag, on a checkered tablecloth in a field where Julie Andrews sings **THE HILLS ARE ALIVE WITH THE SOUND OF MUSIC**, yes, I'm one hundred percent certain that it was written that Wurtzel drank a glass of wine, written in black and white in an article from 2013, an interview Lizzie and the young journalist planned over email, an email where Lizzie wrote in black and white **I AM VERY MUCH A FAN OF WINE AT NOON.** So the young journalist goes to their meeting spot, a restaurant, and—surprise surprise, Lizzie orders wine, the journalist describes the scene in excruciating, unnecessary detail: the sweat glistening on Lizzie's upper lip, the cheese from Lizzie's omelette hanging from her mouth, Lizzie's rambling thoughts illustrated by a stylistic device, **A FOUR-WAY INTERSECTION WITH NO TRAFFIC SIGNAL**, the journalist writes. Actually, now that I'm thinking of the article again, I think the vocabulary used points clearly toward thinly-veiled accusations of madness, yes, the journalist insinuates that Lizzie is what you might call a crazy old lady, an old addict with a fried brain, or other descriptions that make me cry **AGEISM** and **STIGMATIZATION OF MENTAL ILLNESS**. Sometime after that, Elizabeth Wurtzel gave another interview, this time with a writer from *Jezebel*, who went to Lizzie's house to eat crackers with Lizzie, I wonder how one can survive the experience of going to Wurtzel's place, her house full of Springsteen albums, full of framed portraits of herself, full of tears from having recently lost her dog Augusta who was her best friend, yes, the writer went to Lizzie's and once again it seems that Lizzie was **A FAN OF WINE AT NOON** or at any other time of day, the writer describes the red wine that Lizzie drinks and the Percocet that Lizzie takes, yes you read that right, what I'm trying to say is that **NOT ONLY DOES THE FIRST**

DRINK GET YOU DRUNK BUT THE FIRST OPIATES ALSO GET YOU WIRED FOREVER, supporters of the War on Drugs will be happy to read that, even though Lizzie says she doesn't understand why prescription opiates get people addicted to heroin, if there's one person who should understand that it's Lizzie, but anyway, I'm beating around the bush, because here we have an addict who, at the age of thirty-four, wrote a book about addiction, not really self-help, but still, **IT DOESN'T WORK IF YOU DON'T WORK IT**. And now that Lizzie is forty-eight the question is how can you **WORK IT** if you have cancer, because that's what the article's about: Elizabeth Wurtzel discusses her cancer, her most recent battle, a battle throughout which she remains as zen as a yoga instructor, zen like four hundred Percocet tablets, zen, because cancer isn't depression, it isn't the **BLACK WAVE**, it's not nothing but it isn't a big thing for Lizzie either. Anyway, if sick people don't take prescription opiates then who's gonna take them, you have to remember that, you have to understand that it's **DAMNED IF YOU DON'T AND DAMNED IF YOU DO**, how can a person with substance issues survive cancer without taking painkillers I wonder, how can Lizzie stay so calm without taking the emergency exit I wonder, the answer certainly can't be found in that interview nor in Lizzie's mouth or anywhere else, because Lizzie herself says she's a liar, remember: **HOW CAN YOU TELL A JUNKIE IS LYING? HER LIPS ARE MOVING.** Plus, Lizzie contradicts herself when she tells that *Jezebel* writer that **YOU CAN JUST DECIDE ENOUGH IS ENOUGH**, which makes me want to cry because I know that last January Lizzie tweeted **FOR A CERTAIN KIND OF PERSON NOTHING IS EVER ENOUGH.** I agreed with her then and I still do now, it's exactly that kind of statement that makes me love Wurtzel, the kind of statement that the Wurtzel of *Prozac Nation* wrote, the kind of statement that a girl of twenty-seven writes in her first novel, the ever-*Sad Girl*, "Sad Girl Theory is a gesture of research that is structured around the idea that the internalized suffering women experience should be categorized as an act of resistance. [...] Sorrow, weeping, starvation, and eventually suicide have been dismissed as symptoms of mental illness or even pure narcissism for girls. I'm proposing that they are actually active, autonomous, and political as well as devastating."[13] My own personal sad girl, my mirror even if I don't have cancer... anyway last January Lizzie didn't have cancer either, everything changed, inexorably we age, I age, you age, Lizzie ages and it won't be that interview that stops time even if it may slow it, it can be inscribed into Lizzie's agency, the "active re-writing of our lives"[14] that Lizzie participates in, her way of exploring all the little nooks of her illnesses, like for example her depression which could on the surface be seen as a weakness, but is in fact the sign of a force of unshakeable resistance. So we can drink wine, we can eat crackers, we can buy ourselves a new dog, but nothing can stop us from contradicting our past in the future, in the future we'll party and drink, because even if we decide to get back on the straight and narrow when ENOUGH IS ENOUGH, those are only words spoken with a glass in hand

---

13. Yasi Salek, "Audrey Wollen on Sad Girl Theory", *Cultist*, June 19 2014, http://www.cultistzine.com/2014/06/19/cult-talkaudrey-wollen-on-sad-girl-theory/.

14. bell hooks and Jill Soloway, "Ending Domination : The Personal Is Political", *YouTube*, September 7 2016, https://www.youtube.com/watch?v=Fw6Fd87PhjU, 1 min 32 s.

and at least four more forehead lines than we had at 27, so I exclaim that if Lizzie drank a glass of wine, that means **IT DOESN'T WORK IF YOU DON'T WORK IT**. I remember all the words from her tale of addiction, *More Now Again*, I especially remember the end where Lizzie finished the three hundred and twenty-nine pages with a blank page, a symbol of a new beginning, **STARTING FROM ZERO** as Joe Bocan would say, a white symbol like the white feather flying through the blue sky in *Forrest Gump*, a symbol of purity that, thirteen years later, thirteen years after the publication of *More Now Again*, is sullied, like a white DKNY shirt stained with a rosé drank on a patio in the West Village, sullied like the reputation of an author who wrote a book with the subtitle *A Memoir of Addiction*, stained like my conviction that it's possible to one day be okay, abstinent, sober, that it's possible to one day be free from having to shake hands with old people in church basements. This realization of the failure of total abstinence from substances is a stain that spreads in my bathtub while I rinse my hair thinking that I, too, **AM VERY MUCH A FAN OF WINE**

AT NOON, which makes me a liar like Lizzie, an addict like Lizzie, a loser like Lizzie, only, unlike Lizzie, I have no interview, no future book deals, I don't even have a cheese omelette and when I cry out **MORE NOW AGAIN**, it's in the void of my own blank page.

Warning
it's over
OK
OVER
Warning
it's over
Warning
it's over
OK
OVER
OVER
Warning
it's over
OK
OK
Warning
Warning
Warning
it's over
Warning
it's over
OK
OVER
Warning
it's over
OK
Warning
OK
Warning
OK
OVER

SO IT SEEMS that I like to make all my dates carry the burden of the mistakes I've made with my exes, that's how I am, I spit my bitter memories in their faces hoping they won't flinch, as Angelina Jolie said in *Gia*: **THE TRICK IS YOU SCARE THE SHIT OUT OF PEOPLE, THAT WAY THEY DON'T SEE HOW SCARED YOU ARE**, that's the idea, that whoever's the strongest will win and she'll stand up with the *Rocky* theme playing. I say that but I've never seen *Rocky*, I've only seen a queer wrestling match once or twice in my life, fights aren't really my thing, no, my thing is vomiting my stories into my victims' faces knowing full well they'll run away, after all "We live in a society that is embarrassed by interiority"[15] and up to now I have to say it's been working pretty well, everything's going great, I go to bed alone every night smiling just enough to make the corners of my lips crack, I smile as I imagine my future as an old maid who will never live past thirty, it's been planned for a long time, planned since I was six and my babysitter's daughter had looked

---

15. Daphne Merkin, *This Close to Happy: A Reckoning With Depression*, New York, Farrar, Straus and Giroux, 2017, p. 10.

me up and down and finally said ONLY OLD MAIDS WEAR OVERALLS and I had to ask my mom what an old maid was, and honestly, it never seemed all that bad to me, it isn't so bad if you believe *Buzzfeed* and their WHICH CRAZY FEMALE TROPE ARE YOU quiz—I got CRAZY CAT LADY, I could have also gotten FEMINIST KILLJOY, it would have been just as true. "The feminist killjoy 'spoils' the happiness of others; she is a spoilsport because she refuses to convene, to assemble, to meet over happiness,"[16] yes, I love being a killjoy, a party pooper, the bird of ill omen, the token whiner, it's actually interesting that women who write about their personal experiences are so often targets of insults, described as "full of self-pity, self-absorbed, whiny, self-indulgent, LiveJournal-esque, annoying."[17] It's all so maddening, it makes me want to scream the words of Fiona Apple at them: KEEP ON CALLING ME NAMES, KEEP ON, KEEP ON, or the words of Joan Baez: CALL ME ANY NAME YOU LIKE I WILL NEVER DENY IT, you see I'm once again the girl who's all frustrated, the girl

---

16. Sara Ahmed, *op. cit.*, p. 65.
17. "*Prozac Nation* by Elizabeth Wurtzel", *Goodreads*, https://www.goodreads.com/book/show/227603.

who writes in the first person in the hope that her literary confessions might be able to heal, if not myself then others, I hope so, I cherish my first-person I like the flesh of my flesh, that pronoun that is so essential to me, that I use in excess, yes, "The personal pronoun *I* is crucial; it's a site from which we can take stock, take responsibility, and take space if space is needed."[18] I write my *I* in my corner, solitary, alone, wild, which is basically the definition of an old maid, an old maid with a cat in each of the pockets of her overalls. When I was six they called me Marie Four-Pockets even though I actually had six pockets in my jumper. It made me mad, but I wouldn't say anything, not a word, my lips shut tight because I hadn't yet learned to smile, I was content with staying alone and practicing saying nothing, it would have been the perfect moment to try to court me, but it never happened, so I developed the aforementioned technique: I scare people to keep them from loving me, I spit out pieces of the puzzle of my unhappiness between bites as I wine and dine my Tinder date, maybe because I never succeeded in putting all my puzzle

---

18. Erin Wunker, *op. cit.*, p. 29.

pieces together even though I know full well that **MANY HANDS MAKE LIGHT WORK**, like they taught us as kids on Passe-Partout, one day maybe I'll find someone who will be good at problem solving, someone who will be strong enough to spit right back into my face, she'll be the Tyler to my Jack, we'll start our own *Fight Club*, but to find my Tyler I'll need to go through several candidates, my own personal dating show, I want to find the right girl, the one, I'm ready to risk it all, even my own skin, because as Tyler says: **IT'S ONLY AFTER WE'VE LOST EVERYTHING THAT WE'RE FREE TO DO ANYTHING**, it works out well because I've had nothing to lose for a long time now, so I'm ready for anything, I'm ready for her, I'm ready for you, you, you, or you.

MARCH

ONCE AGAIN Angelina Jolie was photographed with her family by Annie Leibovitz, looking happy with Maddox, Zahara, Pax, Shiloh, Vivienne, and Knox, the family smiles at the camera and I smile back at my computer screen, I smile at Angie's face and Angie's words **I CAN'T WAIT TO HIT FIFTY AND KNOW I MADE IT**, because of course these photos are accompanied by an article. I stare at the *Vogue* logo and wonder what the secret to eternal youth could be, the elixir that could make us wake up after thirty years and still be alive and actually be happy about it, be happy every morning feeling the sheets on our body, the pillow on our face, the air on our lips, I mean, how did Angie make it past thirty, how did she do it, I would say **GRADUALLY THEN SUDDENLY**, she probably went from twenty nine to thirty without us noticing, without much fanfare, but we don't really know, maybe she was up all night worrying about how it would go, maybe she panicked as she felt her hair grow, her teeth move, her face sink, maybe she badtripped about the weight of time passing, the hardships she went through that never went well, maybe she even cried, paralyzed in her bed, that coffin without walls that held her prisoner over the last week of her twenties. What did she do to rid herself of that anxiety, maybe she swallowed a couple of Xanax, a couple of Centrum vitamins while staring at the blank wall in front of her, or maybe it was a wall with a mirror on it, she stared into the mirror and saw herself without really seeing herself, her long hair, her wide eyes, her big mouth, seeing all that without really understanding, without understanding anything at all except that time just passes and we can't keep up with it or some other cliché like that. Angie is used to clichés since she was a model at the ripe young age of fourteen, it was her mother who made her pose for the camera while all Angie wanted was to go back into her basement in Malibu to play with her knives, a dangerous but oh-so-interesting activity, one that I know well, there's nothing like the cold blade on the soft sensitive forearm, when we don't know where we're going and why we're running there it's always nice to slow down and feel the weight of time on that blade, don't go thinking that manifestations of suffering are passive acts, I want to reclaim self-harm as a form of agency that turns the body into a site of resistance, even though I know that the blade doesn't forgive, it doesn't forgive anything apart from maybe being young and pretty, don't go believing that what I'm saying isn't feminist, I stand firm in this position, "a feminism grounded in negation, refusal, passivity, absence, and silence, that offers spaces and modes of unknowing, failing, and forgetting as part of an alternative feminist project, a shadow feminism which has nestled in more positivist accounts and unraveled their logics from within,"[19] young like the heroine of a French film, pretty like the heroin that flows in Angie's veins. Yes, I've already told you: Angie doesn't have a past that you could qualify as "easy" or even "common," that's precisely why she's my favourite,

---

19. Jack Halberstam, *The Queer Art of Failure*, Durham, Duke University Press, 2011, p. 124.

the one person who might help me solve the mystery of eternal youth, the one who will save me with photos taken on the seashore—only a mother knows how to be happy, with Maddox, Zahara, Pax, Shiloh, Vivienne, and Knox, while I'm neither a mother nor a whore nor a virgin, nor am I even the woman who can say, **I CAN'T WAIT TO HIT THIRTY AND KNOW I MADE IT.**

I CAN'T WAIT TO HIT 30 AND KNOW I MADE IT

WHEN I MET EILEEN MYLES she told me **YOU'D BE AN EXCELLENT PROSE WRITER, YOU HAVE TOO MUCH TO SAY FOR POETRY**, so I sit in front of my MacBook, I sit in my new work space, a little desk that faces a mirror, a big mirror where I keep one eye on my facial expression when I write or rather my facial expression when I stare at the screen without adding anything at all to my Word documents that are called **SOMEPOEMS.DOC** or **SOME-WORDS.DOC**. I look at myself in the mirror because I'm tired of seeing water pockets under my eyes, tired of seeing myself blurry, half-seeing, I don't feel like the **NEXT GREAT CANADIAN WRITER**, I feel more like Elizabeth Wurtzel, a writer who sacrificed herself, like Nelly Arcan, a novelist who killed herself, but barely, barely, I mean, I'd rather be a fragment of Wurtzel than be me, I'd rather be a piece of Arcan than be me, I mean, after all who will read these words, as Rebecca Solnit writes: "There is no good answer to being a woman."[20] I'll always lose at this game, my own game, the one I jump into with both feet

---

20. Rebecca Solnit, "The Mother of All Questions," *Harper's Magazine*, October 2015, https://harpers.org/archive/2015/10/themother-of-all-questions.

like when we'd play jump rope in the school yard, it's me, Miss Mary Mack all dressed in black, when I met Eileen Myles I mulled over those words in my head, **EXCELLENT PROSE WRITER**, I want to (re)write my life to have a bit of control, I want to erase to better start again, cross it all out to better correct, dissect to better understand. "I am writing this book in an effort to exert some mastery over my own experience by closely observing it,"[21] I swear I'm trying hard, without much success because I say when, I say how, I say why I'm unable to write, to exist through the great void of the end of winter, the winter of a million reads that I hoped would make me want to write, but instead of growing in the wisdom of these great ladies of literature I shriveled up like the tiniest kernel of literary life, a dried up seed that will never sprout, a little seed of nothing that cries in the shadow of the mad women of literary history. I cry as I watch the wall ripple while Charlotte Perkins Gilman and Bertha Mason encourage me to go outside, they tell me to take advantage of a life where I don't weave, a life where I have the

---

21. Daphne Merkin, *op. cit.*, p. 17.

choice to take control of my keyboard and become **AN EXCELLENT PROSE WRITER**.

I'M THINKING OF THE LOVE I LOST, I type her name into Google and my search auto-completes with those unpromising words, "cause of death," a question without a question mark that I know the answer to, even if I'd rather forget, even if I can't say with certainty because everyone around her kept their mouths shut, her parents said **SHE DIED IN HER SLEEP** and her friends echoed them, but the elephant in the room, the elephant wearing a tutu because after all she did ballet—for years she did classical dance, wishing for a brittle body—the elephant in the room is that everyone knew she lived dangerously, the proof is in the hundreds of tearful emails where she talked to me about retox and I would dive head-first into the game, I would describe my own poisons, we would write to each other alone in our beds, hers in Boston, mine in Montreal, on Google Chat, Facebook Chat, SMS, always in contact, because it's by insidiously digging her claws into me that she knew how to keep me close to her despite the distance. I never would have imagined that out of the two of us it would be her who won the bet of becoming a rock star, but it makes sense, it's to be expected, she had already met Debbie Harry, Cyndi Lauper, and Madonna, she who befriended all the big stars to appropriate a bit of their celebrity, she lived by proxy and so did I, actually, in that regard. I understand her perfectly, an entire life coming up with scripts worthy of the best Hollywood movies, the most extravagant American music videos. In short, she died at the age of twenty-seven. I don't know if I'll ever stop thinking of her, the love of my life, because I've already made it past twenty-seven, the year when I could have potentially caught up to her, the year when I turned the same age she was when she died, the year when every day that went by made me a little older than her, which is strange because she was older than me, but that's normal: when we die, we stop aging, we become a number forever, if that number is twenty-seven then we become iconic, we enter the select club that includes Janis Joplin, Amy Winehouse, Kurt Cobain and all the others, so if we live past twenty-seven, we die at an ordinary age, a number just like any other that isn't part of any sort of club. In grief there is anger and sadness, which are basic emotions, but there are also nuanced emotions that are more complex, like resentment, longing, bitterness, regret, along with other little emotions that resurge when we least expect it, that surprise us when we stumble onto a deserted Instagram account, an abandoned Facebook page, or even old Gmail chat logs that you thought had been erased, every day I live some kind of emotion for her, the love of my life, always a different feeling, but often not all that complex. What I mean is, I feel a lot of regret, mainly regret, every day regret, because she and I are a really clichéd story that I'm hesitant to include within another, that's why I've chosen poetry, **WORDS TEND TO BE INADEQUATE**, says Jenny Holzer, who also says **OFFER VERY LITTLE INFORMATION ABOUT YOURSELF**, which is exactly what my lost love did; the truth about her eludes me. The truth, really, is that I can offer no explanations, she was twenty-seven and then suddenly she was dead, just like I'll be thirty and then suddenly I'll be dead.

APRIL

I LOOKED AT ELIZABETH WURTZEL'S TWITTER PAGE AGAIN because I wanted to remember her exact words about emptiness, the BLACK WAVE, the definition of limits, something like, FOR A CERTAIN KIND OF PERSON, ENOUGH IS NEVER ENOUGH, I told myself that if I'm quoting Lizzie I want to do it perfectly, it's pretty obvious that I'm obsessed with the idea of perfection, in any form, at any hour of the day, I can't allow myself to fail, especially when it comes to words, and particularly when it comes to Lizzie's, nothing has changed with time, nothing at all, because it's always the same story, Marie-Sissi Labrèche would understand, she'd be laughing hard with beer all around her mouth, she'd understand Lizzie who would understand, too. But anyway, I didn't find the exact quote, on Elizabeth Wurtzel's Twitter page I only found a link to a *Vice* article where Lizzie tells us about her cancer in the same way she'd tell us that she bought a turquoise ring in a little brick and mortar shop on the Upper West Side. Lizzie allows herself the luxury of laughing at cancer, because cancer isn't depression, it isn't cutting your legs with a pocket knife in the girls' locker room, it isn't kicking everyone out of the party because the cat puked on the pile of coats, it isn't being holed up in a seedy room in Florida marathoning old episodes of *SVU*, it isn't writing for *Rolling Stone* while snorting Ritalin off the back of a Bruce Springsteen CD case—it isn't that, it isn't that at all, but it isn't nothing either—anyway only Lizzie could say, **COMPARED WITH BEING TWENTY-SIX AND CRAZY AND WAITING FOR SOME GUY TO CALL, CANCER IS NOT SO BAD.** Lizzie knows what she's talking about after all, cancer is just another hurdle, a trough of the **BLACK WAVE**, nothing insurmountable, Lizzie says: "People think I am writing about myself. But really I am writing about everybody, because I am just like everybody else. We are all so alike,"[22] and that's when Sylvia Plath cheers

---

22. Elizabeth Wurtzel, "People think I am writing about myself.

in encouragement from her grave, she who was so often the figurehead of so-called confessional poetry, meanwhile I'm wondering: women's confessional poetry, is that redundant? Confessional—that's me, you, him, her, we write about our life experiences, as Chris Kraus said in an interview: "The things that happen to me are things that happen to everybody. They're not unique. So to talk about them candidly—there's nothing confessional about it."[23] Repeat after me: **I AM ORDINARY**! That's how Lizzie's words connect with Angie's, since she's also a cancer survivor, she also watched her mother die of cancer, Lizzie and Angie will show each other their new breasts while drinking wine, **IT'S THE FIRST DRINK THAT GETS YOU DRUNK**, but it wouldn't really matter anymore, because after all what's a glass of wine when you're forty-eight, a glass of wine isn't an eightball bought in the backseat of a black Audi, a glass of wine isn't a bag from Walgreens full of orange prescription

---

But really I am writing about everybody, because I am just like everybody else. We are all so alike," *Twitter*, April 6 2017, https://twitter.com/LizzieWurtzel/status/850136012844040192.
23. Leslie Jamison, "Chris Kraus," *Interview Magazine*, July 17 2017, https://www.interviewmagazine.com/culture/chris-kraus.

containers, a glass of wine isn't an apartment floor covered in multicoloured baggies, no, a glass of wine is for celebrating, it's reserved for partying, toasting to the triumph of overcoming illness, marking the time that goes by but never goes well, giving a toast while I add a new mantra to my collection: **FOR A CERTAIN KIND OF PERSON, NOTHING IS EVER ENOUGH, NOT EVEN FUCKING CANCER.**

Recherches associées   Afficher 10 autres éléments

Erik Skjoldbjærg   Sylvia Plath   Susanna Kaysen   Lucy Grealy   Anne Sexton

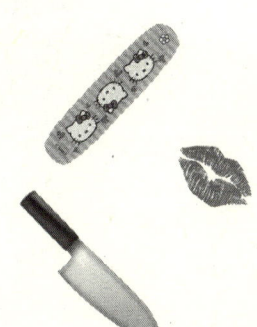

ANGELINA JOLIE HAS OFFICIALLY ANNOUNCED that she had a preventative mastectomy as well as a preventative ovarian ablation, basically, preventative procedures to fight an imaginary illness, I mean, an illness that isn't one yet, but since the idea is there and the money is there too then why not. Note that I am not saying that to criticize her, I love her, I love to obsess about a body that isn't my own, I'm watching all of Angelina Jolie's movies and I get an email from my mom that says she's in the middle of watching Macha Grenon die on TV. My mom writes to me, "Why do the dead always look so serene on TV, when in real life they're anything but." It's true that in movies and TV everything is easier, death is a release, a relief, a catharsis for the living who stay at the bedside of the dying, who tell themselves, "Yes, Macha was a very good mother, sister, wife, friend, employee, citizen," Macha was all that, just like you and me sitting here staring at our screens, imagining a future where stories repeat themselves one after another, a variation on the same theme. TV taught me that, too, at a young age with **THE CIRCLE OF LIFE** and **THE NEVERENDING STORY**,

I wonder now what that has left me with, if not a few words I've heard a thousand times before, clichés to encourage me to stay, I tell myself **IF I MADE IT THROUGH ___ THEN I CAN GET THROUGH ___, WHAT DOESN'T KILL YOU MAKES YOU STRONGER** Kanye would say. An army of girls confined to their rooms, their beds, their pathos—**YOU ARE THE WOUND** Lena Dunham screamed in the show *Girls*—I calmly acquiesce, I'm the open wound, I am post-wounded: "a shift away from wounded affect,"[24] what does that mean, it means you just need to calmly accumulate experiences like as many chapters or scenes as you need to properly construct your book or movie, the heroines need to get through their ordeals, Elizabeth Wurtzel taught me that, Elizabeth Wurtzel the literary queen of pathos whom we love to throw insults at. "We" doesn't include the present speaker obviously, not me, no, I prefer to drink Lizzie's words like an alcoholic who can't put down the bottle, every day I go look at Lizzie's Twitter account, every day I quench my thirst with her words like a phony prophecy from a gas station per-

---

24. Leslie Jamison, , *op. cit.*, p. 198.

sonal growth book, we have to fuel up when we can, we have to keep moving forward, for whom, for what, for whatever you want, whether it's Angie, Macha, or Lizzie, we have the idols that are available to us, we have the pathos we want, we have to stay up to date on the lives of celebrities in fiction and real life because just like them we live in the public sphere. We feed the camera's eye without thinking of what will become of these images that will eventually be archives, we base our decisions on what Angie, Macha, or Lizzie are living, without really analyzing it, without controlling anything, which brings us back to: there's no point in planning ahead—it's better to die when we're ready.

MAY

I HAVE A NEW STRATEGY. Today I went to the optometrist and I chose contact lenses. No, not purple lenses like the ones I wore in grade 10 when the little boys would call me a witch, no, this time I chose grown-up contact lenses, clear and disposable lenses because as Debbie Harry sings ALL I WANT IS 20-20 VISION, A TOTAL PORTRAIT WITH NO OMISSIONS, all I want is to get better and stop crying, good thing that's what contacts are for, contacts are for stopping me from crying because I'm already barely capable of tolerating them, crying with my contacts in is even worse, it makes me feel like my eyes are melting, so that's how it'll work, it'll work like a conditioned response, every time I'll want to cry it'll hurt so I'll stop myself. Like earlier: I was driving with my new contacts in and when Liz Phair sang IT'S TRUE THAT I STOLE YOUR

LIGHTER, IT'S ALSO TRUE THAT I LOST THE MAP. I thought of my lost love, of the passing of time, I wanted to cry, I felt the tears form, and right away it hurt, my vision blurred and I thought "I have to stop crying if I don't want to crash," but that's the thing, that's where my plan is dangerous, because maybe deep down I do want to crash, maybe deep down I want to cry while it hurts because I'm used to it and I'm not one of Pavlov's dogs, I never learn from my mistakes or my pain, I've never learned anything at all even though I finished my university studies—well, alright, I did learn a few lessons, like for example I learned that in life you can't give yourself too much shit, so fuck everyone who tells me to persevere. As soon as I got home I looked up toward the sky like I do a thousand times a day, I pinched my cornea to take my contacts out, one less tear barrier, now I can cry as much as I want while I listen to Liz Phair or Debbie Harry or even as I watch *A Clockwork Orange*. I tell myself that it's okay to feel pain, it's okay to cry, anyway I have sixty pairs of contacts to practice with, let me poke myself in the eye again and maybe one day I'll learn my lesson.

WHEN I'M NOT binge-eating coconut Clif bars at eleven at night, I read Michelle Tea's autobiography, a book that's a very fast read, in fact I'm not surprised at all by my literary excitement since Michelle Tea is my favourite author after Eileen Myles, after Elizabeth Wurtzel, after all the others, yes, Michelle Tea is my favourite. I guess that's pretty predictable because it seems like the only authors that interest me are addicts or ex-addicts, I'm as predictable as a girl who's been eating the same granola bars for ten years, like a girl who's been repeating the same mistakes for ten years, like a girl who doesn't know how to stop being a girl and become a woman— actually, as it happens, Michelle Tea's book is called **HOW TO GROW UP**, like a secret recipe situated somewhere between autobiography and self-help book, like a story that starts off badly but ends well, like a little girl watching Disney movies in hopes of finding Prince Charming, like a woman reading a book in hopes of finding relief, because if Michelle Tea can go from an apartment with cockroaches in the fridge to a house with a patio by the sea then I can too, if Michelle Tea can go from glimmering crystal meth to sparkling Perrier then I can too, I can do anything I want if I count the days I have left, but first I'll start by finishing this book, this book in which Michelle Tea touches on a few issues, since it's a particular feature of the intimate narrative to dress wounds before an audience that will cry out **ME TOO, ME TOO**. It's a particular feature of that kind of narrative to lick one's wounds before a delirious crowd that can't let go of their traumas, the crowd screams **WE ARE THE WOUND**, the crowd even brandishes signs with slogans like **SUFFERING AS A DRIVING FORCE OF CREATION or TRAUMATIZED AND LITERARY**, those who don't understand will never understand, they can spit their disdain on a Goodreads page with their **IF I COULD GIVE THIS BOOK ZERO STARS I WOULD**, we literary traumatized girls won't give a shit, it's important to do it for yourself, **GO ON DO IT FOR YOURSELF** like the blue man said in the ad, or not, or not, maybe we have to write without reason, "I don't write for healing, or for rescuing myself or being rescued by literature. I don't write *for*."[25] It's important to read

---

25. France Théoret, *Journal pour mémoire*, Montréal, L'Hexagone,

all the pages up to the end and not to be shy about highlighting things, make the pages go from white to yellow or whatever other colour, if you don't understand don't even bother reading books, reading my books, **TALK TO MY HAND**, this hand that's busy typing. I'll read **HOW TO GROW UP** right up to the last page, up to the last chapter where Michelle Tea writes, "In my twenties I became aware of a curious distinction: there were people who were 'in' their bodies and there were people who were not 'in' their bodies,"[26] and that's exactly it, that's where I got excited once again before the magic of the mirror that is writing, because I've often reflected on "not being in my body," I've never been in my body, I wasn't in my body when I did ballet in my extra-small pink leotard, I wasn't in my body when I was testing my art supplies out on my forearms, I wasn't in my body when I let people inside it, I wasn't in my body for twenty-nine years of this life of a ghost who hears you scream **GLORY TO THE GYM** while depression isn't an exclusively physiological

---

1993, p. 15, free translation.
26. Michelle Tea, *How To Grow Up*, New York, Penguin, 2015, p. 275.

condition, "Depression should be viewed as a social and cultural phenomenon, not a biological and medical one,"[27] you cry *gym* like it's cure-all for any ailment, *gym* from the mouths of doctors, dietitians, psychologists, psychiatrists, experts of all sorts, a beautiful suggestion from beautiful people who are fine **"IN" THEIR BODIES**, beautiful people who don't know what it's like to be outside of it, a tourist, a spectator, Scully in *X-Files* watching the flying saucer land, **THE TRUTH IS OUT THERE**, the truth is somewhere inside me, but where exactly, I'll have to dig. One day I'll have to inhabit my abandoned body, I'll have to dig with grapefruit spoons into my pink flesh, it'll be a huge undertaking, I'll have to buy gum, it'll be a labour that requires several years of research because I really do have to find a way to fill the void, so in the meantime I gorge myself on coconut Clif bars at eleven at night, because for now it's by filling my stomach that I manage to inhabit myself.

---

27. Ann Cvetkovich, *Depression: A Public Feeling*, Durham, Duke University Press, 2013, p. 88.

I DON'T KNOW HOW TO BEGIN to tell to you that Lizzie got married, yes, proof of the passing of time. I'd like to ask her how she went from depressed to married, I want to know if we can really rid ourselves of the **BLACK WAVE** or if it'll always sneak its way back in, if depression is a social and cultural phenomenon, how to heal from it in a world whose values don't correspond to our own. Can we really talk about healing, anyway, there's probably only one thing left to do: "Turn illness into a weapon,"[28] use depression as a form of resistance against instances of oppression, but I don't know where to start, all I know is that when I like Lizzie's wedding photos I'm just one fan among many, even if I write **I AM SO HAPPY FOR YOU LIZZIE** I'm just another Instagram follower among a thousand others, nothing exceptional, **TELL ME WHAT IS SO EXCEPTIONAL ABOUT LIZZIE** Andrée Watters asks me—well it's simple: Lizzie is a survivor, a fighter, while I'm just annoying, a young girl in tears, because I'm telling you, this whole passing of time thing is really starting to weigh on me. I didn't want to admit

---

28. Amy Berkowitz, *op. cit.*, p. 32.

it but in a month and a half I'll have been writing for a year, I've been documenting, I've been counting down every minute of this last year of existence, a whole year of writing to Lizzie without her answering me, a life spent writing without getting an answer, from whom, from what, a year later I'm just a year older, but not a year wiser, the more things change the more they stay the same because nothing really changes. I'll go to my thirtieth birthday party with a smile on my face, a flower crown on my head, a notary on my arm, I'll have to make this milestone official, another year, I'll have to write it down somewhere, they can write it on my arm, tattoo the number the way Angie has geographical coordinates on hers, I'll have signs of the passing of time not just around my eyes but on my whole body as well, numbers tattooed in an intimate ceremony, the notary will lean over me and engrave these numbers into my flesh: a three and a zero. Everyone will applaud, but I'll tell them to stop because it won't be over, while I'm at it I'd like all of my skin to be reddened and blackened with numbers, I'll have them put my number of Twitter Facebook Instagram followers, they'll put their heart into it, they'll put all the energy I was missing through my twenty-ninth year of life into it, they'll push really hard so it'll be indelible and even if it starts to rain from my eyes I'll say **KEEP GOING, KEEP GOING,** we really need to document the passing of time, I don't care if it hurts, I don't care about being dirty, I just want to leave a mark and if I can't leave it on the world, I'll leave that mark on my own skin. Wedding bells and all my best wishes to Lizzie and to myself, as I symbolically marry the passing of time, tattooed in the indelible ink of my wretched age.

EVEN THOUGH IT'S OBVIOUS THAT I ROMANTICIZE MY DEPRESSION, that still doesn't mean that I want to end up on an episode of *Intervention*. The mirror in front of my desk throws my image back at me as I lean over the thin jagged lines on the back of a feminist theory book, I half-open the window and blow out the smoke from my cigarette that hangs from the corner of my lips, I love to indulge in my vices, to be honest, I even do a little dance every time I get up from my chair after drinking, I act like Beyoncé when really I'm Lindsay Lohan—by the way, if I were asked I don't even know if I'd say yes to the Betty Ford Clinic, to Remuda Ranch Florida, to the Sunset Center of Healing, I don't know if I'd dare to do it for myself, who exactly I would decide to get better for, but don't go thinking I never made any effort in that sense. On the contrary, my whole life is therapy, one long analysis where I dissect the causes of my sorrow without ever really putting my finger on the nature of my wound, that gaping wound that changes its place every day. All of my flesh is raw, without clothes, without skin, without a shell, without armour, without anything at all to protect me from a life that attacks me from all sides, my entire being is a wound, **I AM THE WOUND**, I know it, I carry my great sorrow like Félix Leclerc sings about his happiness. My great sorrow and I are inseparable, cats staring at you through the pet shop window, a two-for-one sale at Ardène, the twins in *The Shining*, yes, my sorrow and I are together forever, a toxic union that's impossible to undo, even if you're sitting in my kitchen begging me to act, even if you implore me to take my life into my own hands or whatever expression that's meaningless to me, even if you torment me with your magical thinking and your good intentions, even if you try to convince me with your self-help books and your guided meditation YouTube videos, while I know full well that it's a lost cause, I know all about loss, if there's one thing I'm sure of it's that loss is here to stay, my sorrow doesn't want to go away. "How do we talk about these wounds without glamorizing them?"[29] That's the question and even if it's obvious that I romanticize my sorrow, that still doesn't mean I'm ready to make an appearance on the *Maury Show*,

---

29. Leslie Jamison, *op. cit.*, p. 187.

no, in terms of help, at the most, what I would be willing to do would be to open myself up to you on paper, like a cut, an incision bringing to light my existential emptiness. You'll lean over the operating table, saying, like they said to Lizzie, **SHE WAS SO FULL OF PROMISE**, but the only thing I'll promise you is that I'll be gone one day, soon, I can feel it, I'll erase myself in the void of my thirtieth birthday, I just have to wait for the right moment, a few months, a few days, a few minutes, **SLOWLY BUT SURELY**, inexorably.

wound

Recherche Google J'ai de la chance

●●●○○ Bell LTE 8:39 AM 8%
‹ Messages **Girl** Details

WOUND!

iMessage Send

YOU
ARE
THE
WOUND

Update Status | Add Photos/Video | Create Photo Album

I AM A BIG UGLY FUCKING WOUND

Girls Season 1 Episode 9 fight clip
Hanna and Marnie fight

YOUTUBE.COM

Friends ▾ Post

Hey girl
You are the wound

| No | Yes | I am the wound |

JUNE

Again today I have the urge to tweet at Elizabeth Wurtzel, because as she so aptly put it, FOR A CERTAIN KIND OF PERSON, ENOUGH IS NEVER ENOUGH: that really is me, me who always wants more, me repeating the same mistakes until my death, that's nothing new. Today I'm wondering once again what Lizzie is doing, where she is, how she's doing, but most of all I'm wondering if the BLACK WAVE she describes in PROZAC NATION ever goes away, if it's possible to ever rid yourself of it completely or if the wave always returns, always ready to drown us, me who hates going swimming. When I was little I had *Little Mermaid* floaties, I would wear them in the pool—once at a hotel I jumped into the water, I started swimming and everything was going great until my dad said, "Marie you don't have your floaties," and I started to cry, it was instantaneous, I was going to start sinking, I was done for. Today I was supposed to go to the spa, but since the weather was sort of uncertain I opted for the poor man's spa, also known as the Jarry pool, but as I was arriving I almost rammed into a family who were on their way to the Rogers Cup. Just at that same moment it started to rain, I was talking to myself, I was swearing in front of the kids, but I didn't care because all I wanted was to cry about my cancelled spa day in the chlorinated water of the Jarry pool, the only one in Montreal that has a little corner of grass just at the edge of the concrete, but since it was raining, I went home thinking that the **BLACK WAVE** had taken the form of a shower of cold rain, I thought **WWLD, WHAT WOULD LIZZIE DO**—Lizzie was probably under the sun in the Bahamas with a little umbrella in her drink to celebrate her forty-eighth birthday, actually I'm not sure if she was sober like Eileen Myles, sober in her tropical destination for successful authors, she probably wasn't thinking of the **BLACK WAVE** anymore, that's why I wanted to ask her how to get rid of the darkness even though black is my favourite colour.

When I got home I avoided turning my computer on, instead of tweeting I did an arts and crafts project in my kitchen to take my mind off things, I cut up the ELLE magazine with Angie on the cover, and now Angie is on my kitchen wall watching me eat egg sandwiches, Saint Angie is watching over me now and up till the time of my death, my death which I'm hoping won't come right away, because I'm still waiting for Elizabeth Wurtzel to respond to all the tweets I've sent her over the past year, I've been swimming against the current waiting for her answer, I'm fighting hard and I'm telling myself it would be going a lot better if I had floaties.

I SUDDENLY WANT TO SCREAM because today Christmas came early: Elizabeth Wurtzel finally liked one of my tweets. I was watching the rain fall outside, the emptiness inside me was being filled with an icy cold, minute by minute, and I felt the **BLACK WAVE** coming, I couldn't resist, I succumbed, I opened my desk drawer, the one full of receipts from the Renaissance at the Plaza, the one with the little Jean Coutu bag full of supplies: straws, baggies empty or full, knife, rolled up five dollar bills, paper, pipe, lighter, France Théoret book stained with white powder residue. I drew two thick lines, glancing a couple of times at myself in the mirror that overlooks my desk, while Adele belted out **SOMEONE LIKE YOUUUUUU**, I snorted the two lines in two quick sniffs. My eyes welled up with tears even though I don't cry anymore, not anymore, I'm in a desert break, an unsweetened Kit Kat break, I'd like to cry, I'm a tears specialist, but I don't anymore, not since Effexor, Wellbutrin, Zoloft, Abilify, Lamictal, Prozac, I don't cry anymore since my mood is regulated by pills I swallow morning and night. In short, my eyes watered all of a sudden and when I glanced at my phone that was vibrating I saw the blurry notification: ELIZABETH WURTZEL LIKED YOUR TWEET. I closed one eye, then the other, a few drips fell on the smooth surface of my iPhone and I realized what happened: a few minutes earlier, I had quoted Lizzie in a tweet talking about how she saw her pills, her drugs, a quote taken from her book *More Now Again*: "They are my sugar, they are the sweetness in the days that have none, they drip through me like tupelo honey, then they are gone, then I need more, I always need more, for all my life I have needed more."[30] Sometimes when I read Lizzie, or Nelly, or Marie-Sissi, I get discouraged and I get the urge to throw the book I'm holding across the room, into the garbage, because I can't stand the idea that in my writing all I do is repeat what's already been said, said better, by the women who came before me, we don't reinvent anything, the wheel keeps turning, but I really like sticking my finger into it, my whole hand into the spokes, diving elbow-deep into the wound. I torture myself trying to write

---

30. Elizabeth Wurtzel, *More Now Again: A Memoir of Addiction*, New York, Simon & Schuster, 2003, p. 3.

what's been said a thousand times before, I develop arguments that allow the existence of a space where being "unhappy[31]" is a political choice or a freedom to take, among an army of crazy girls fighting to be heard, a crowd of ungovernable warriors fighting every second to survive, just one more minute, we want to stay alive just a little longer, long enough for a few screams or a few tweets, enough to fall into excess just before being extinguished completely, we always want more, **FOR ALL OUR LIVES WE HAVE NEEDED MORE.**

---

31. Sara Ahmed, *The Promise of Happiness*, op. cit.

I HAVE A STIFFNESS IN MY HAND FROM WRITING, a lump in my throat from talking, a hole in my heart from crying. The reason for my sorrow is simple, it's coming, I can see it coming outside among the mattresses piling up on the sidewalk: the first of July is on our doorstep, the first of July and I'll be a year older than I was last year, it makes sense, yet it's what I wanted to avoid. I wanted time to be suspended over this last year of my life, I wanted a break, a reprieve, a magic trick, but there it is, **SLOWLY BUT SURELY** said the tortoise to the hare, **GRADUALLY THEN SUDDENLY** said Lizzie, I blinked and a year passed, I closed my eyes and a year went by, I barely had time to see it happen because I was busy chasing after the carrot, the rabbit, the gift that made me run in circles on my track for a year. I documented this last year, a whole year spent watching life run out, collapse on itself, a whole year spent counting down the days with Abilify or Zoloft, prescription and non-prescription drugs, having fun or not having fun, being sad or not being sad, trying not to succumb to the melancholy of the **BLACK WAVE**, learning to surf to the rhythm of dialogues with Nelly, Lizzie, Angie, Marie-Sissi, I felt like I was inhabiting these souls that weren't mine by writing everything but happiness, which is an abstract concept that I've enjoyed reassessing: "I write from a position of skeptical disbelief in happiness as a technique for living well."[32] Happiness is a cup of tea with which to tell the future while I cry again and again on my iPhone, on all my screens, I cry to dilute my life where Angie's face slowly fades at the dawn of my thirtieth birthday that will evaporate like magic because I told you: I'm a witch, my thirtieth birthday will go by quick like a white line up Lizzie's nose. My needle oscillates on the dashboard of my life, one day I want to die and the next I want to play, I tell myself that I can probably wait another year, **I THINK I'LL WAIT ANOTHER YEAR**, Amanda Palmer sings that, I'll wait until I'm even more depressed, I'll endure, I'll cry, I'll push myself to the edge of the **BLACK WAVE** and then abruptly sink—they say you have to hit **ROCK BOTTOM** if you truly want to rise again. I think that'll be a detail that will drag me into the trough of the wave, one day we're alive

---

32. Sara Ahmed, *op. cit.*, p. 2.

and the next we're not, it's easy: **I HAVE MY NEW BILL HICKS CD / I HAVE MY FRIENDS AND MY CAREER / I THINK I'LL WAIT ANOTHER YEAR**, I'll wait for another year when I won't buy myself any CDs, a year when I'll really want to leave, that year could be tomorrow like it could be in ten years, slowly but surely I became a doomed woman who fantasizes about her own death, like Winona Ryder in *Girl, Interrupted*: **YOU MAKE A STUPID REMARK, YOU KILL YOURSELF; YOU LIKE THE MOVIE OF THE WEEK, YOU'LL LIVE**; I hang onto details knowing that one day I could easily swing the other way, the slightest comment will make me waver, tomorrow or in ten years, I know full well that when there won't be any space left to pile up the mattresses on the sidewalk my time will have come, I feel the expiry date coming, my calendar is marked with a line in red ink, a cut, that morning when I won't wake up, it'll be your turn to have a lump in your throat when you learn that I finally gave up, the only thought that will console you is that I'll have finally joined my sisters in suffering so we can talk about what it means to resist.

REFRAINS

(In order of appearance in the text)

Fiona Apple, "Extraordinary Machine" (song)
Elizabeth Wurtzel, *Prozac Nation* (book)
Drake, "Hold On We're Coming Home" (song)
Cat Power, "Good Woman" (song)
Hole, "Doll Parts" (song)
David Lynch, *Inland Empire* (film)
James Mangold, *Girl, Interrupted* (film)
Joan Baez, "Farewell Angelina" (song)
Kathleen, "Ça va bien" (song)
Gertrude Stein, "Sacred Emily" (poem)
Jefferson Airplane, "White Rabbit" (song)
Garbage, "Only Happy When It Rains" (song)
Bruno Pelletier, "Aime" (song)
Céline Dion, "On ne change pas" (song)
Joan Didion, *Play it as It Lays* (book)
Ace of Base, "Beautiful Life" (song)
Brigitte Fontaine, "Conne" (song)
Elizabeth Wurtzel, *More Now Again* (book)

Julie Andrews, "The Hills Are Alive" (song)
Collectif, *Big Book* (book)
Joe Bocan, "Repartir à zéro" (song)
Michael Cristofer, *Gia* (film)
Fiona Apple, "Get Gone" (song)
Laurent Lachance, *Passe-Partout* (television series)
David Fincher, *Fight Club* (film)
Jenny Holzer, "Truisms" (visual installation)
Roger Allers and Rob Minkoff, *The Lion King* (film)
Wolfgang Petersen, *The Neverending Story* (film)
Kanye West, "Stronger" (song)
Lena Dunham, *Girls* (television series)
Blondie, "Picture This" (song)
Liz Phair, "Divorce Song" (song)
Chris Carter, *X-Files* (television series)
Andrée Watters, "Si exceptionnel" (song)
Adele, "Someone Like You" (song)
Amanda Palmer, "Another Year" (song)

NATALIA HERO

Natalia Hero is a Montreal-based writer and literary translator. Her debut novella *Hum*, published in 2018 by Metatron Press, is now available in French as *Colibri* (Marchand de feuilles, 2020). She is the translator of *In the End They Told Them All to Get Lost* by Laurence Leduc-Primeau (QC Fiction, 2019).

MARIE DARSIGNY

Marie Darsigny is an author, poet, artist, and publisher living in Montréal, QC. Educated in literature at Concordia University and UQAM, she is co-editor of the literary platform Filles Missiles. She is the author of the poetry collections *A Little Death Around the Heart* (Metatron Press, 2014) and *Filles* (Écrou, 2017), and the novels *Encore* (2023, Les éditions remue-ménage) and *Trente* (2018, Les éditions remue-ménage).